THE WOMAN was staked out on the ground in a spread-eagled attitude. Face up and by force sexually submissive in a way that her legs were held wide apart and her arms were trapped far to the sides. But she was wearing more clothing than the two Indian braves who were crouched on their haunches at a small fire some fifteen feet away from the helpless captive. Which was a situation Adam Steele found mildly intriguing when he first rode the chestnut mare into a position from where he was able to view the scene clearly.

This in the afternoon shadow of a grotesquely eroded outcrop of sandstone on the ridge of a barren hill. Having moved from the exposed to the shaded side of the slab of rock to make use of its scant cover and so that he could watch the trio over a different angle - his vision unimpaired by the shimmering heat and slow drifting smoke of the brushwood fire.

The Virginian had at first smelled the smoke of the fire as he rode at a leisurely pace along the smooth bed of an arroyo that cut a north to south course through the Big Maria Mountains of southern California. And followed his nose up from the arroyo and across a rugged-surfaced but shallow-inclined slope to the gargoyle like rock at the highest point on the ridge. The acrid taint of the woodsmoke and the stale odour of his own body were the only smells in his nostrils as he rode across the barren slope. Earlier he had been aware, too, of the animal scents of his mount. And now he scowled as he acknowledged that he stank worse than his horse after so many long days and short nights on the slow trek southwards. Or perhaps, because he was the kind of man he was, he merely imagined he smelled worse if he got close to other people less fastidious about such things, he would smell sweet in comparison with the mare.

Then the scowl became briefly more firmly fixed upon his face as he dismissed the implication that it matter what other people thought of him. Next lost the scowl and was impassive when he reined the horse to a halt on the ridge and saw the smoking fire, the two Indian braves and the captive woman. Remained on the totally exposed side of the outcrop for just a second or so before he backed the mare off the skyline and moved her cautiously around to the sun-shaded flank of the rock. Where he was momentarily puzzled by the lack of interest of the braves in their helpless prisoner, while for this same fleeting moment he saw the woman in her enforced posture as nothing more than an object of lust.

But then he scowled again, and matched the expression with a grunt of self-disgust as he had to consciously make himself be objective while he raked a cool-eyed gaze over the scene in its entirety. And moved his right hand away from his left which held the reins, to fist around the frame of the Colt Hartford rifle that was slid into the forward hung boot.

The ridge which was his vantage point was the most westerly of any consequence in the Big Maria range, forming the eastern limit of an area of part undulating and part pool table flat scrub desert that extended to what he guessed were the Little Maria Mountains some ten to fifteen miles away. Mesquite and sasguaro, cottonwood and ocotillo, sagebrush and greasewood grew out on the flatland between the barren high grounds. There were sure to be some wild creatures which survived out there by preying on each other. Above the area, against a blue sky featured with small, stark white clouds, an eagle was circling at high altitude. Or perhaps it was a buzzard. The only sign of man's intrusion on the region was the ugly scene about five hundred feet from where Adam Steele sat unmoving in the saddle of his immobile horse.

The two Indians had made their camp at the base of the quite steep drop from the outcrop-featured ridge for the very good reason that there was a waterhole there. Where they and their pair of burros had refreshed themselves after trekking to this place from the south – leaving sign in the dust and sand to show that each burro had carried a rider and somebody had walked behind: here and there was dragged, when exhaustion refused to be denied. And it was obvious from her dishevelled state, if not from the fact that she was a prisoner, that it was the woman who had walked and been dragged. It looked, too, the way her face was powdered with sweat-tacky dust over ingrained dirt, that she had not been allowed to dip her head into the waterhole and drink.

Whether she was good looking or homely under the grime of long and arduous travel it was not possible to see from such a distance. But she certainly had a fine build, clear to the eye from the tight fit of her pants and shirt that contoured every rise and indentation of her torso and limbs. She was tall for a woman, and had long, slender legs. Her breasts were large and conical: looked youthfully firm.

Once again the Virginian vented a self-deprecating grunt, and needed to will himself to shift the centre of his attention away from the black-clad and black haired woman. To concentrate to the same extent upon the two Indians, who looked like Apaches. About thirty years old, dressed only in undecorated breechclouts, weapons belts, moccasins and headbands with a single eagle feather at the rear. Mean looking, copper complexioned men with muscular builds who, Steele guessed, had endured a long and hard time of deprivation before they struck lucky.

The woman had been just part of their spoils and they had no use for her yet. First had need of the burros with the Mexican style saddles to reach this waterhole on the fringe of the Big Maria Mountains. Where they had staked out their captive to await their pleasure. While they refreshed themselves and the animals, which were then hobbled in the scant shade of a cottonwood to one side of the waterhole. Then the brushwood was collected and the fire was lit, and food was set to cooking in pots – the ingredients of the meal and the utensils used to cook it taken from the packs carried by the burros. This on the other side of the waterhole, downwind from where the gentlest of hot breezes caused the smoke to drift. The braves as unshaded from the blistering heat of the sun as was the woman, but uncaring about this familiar discomfort as they squatted on their haunches and gorged themselves on fiery-smelling chili washed down with strong coffee. Talking and laughing – about their good fortune, perhaps – and totally ignoring the captive woman. As oblivious to her as they were to everything else about their surroundings: including the lone horseman on the ridge above and slightly to the north of them.

After the Virginian had seen that the saddles and accoutrements carried by the burros had a Mexican style to them and then smelled the chili being cooked and eaten, he glanced back at the spreadeagled woman. And decided from the jet blackness of her very long hair and the not so easy to see bone structure of her filthy and anguished face that she had Hispanic blood in her veins.

Then activity close to the fire drew the focus of his attention back to the Indians and he saw that the mid-afternoon meal was over. Tin mugs and plates were simply hurled to the ground as the braves came up off their haunches. The woman sensed from the abrupt ending of the talk and laughter that the period of being left alone to dwell on the hopelessness of her situation was ended. And she snapped open her eyes and turned her head so she could see her captors. Continued to stare at them, wall-eyed and seemingly incapable of experiencing any kind of emotion any more as, after they had taken the cooking and coffee pots off the fire, they clawed aside their breechclouts to expose themselves and urinate into the spluttering flames.

The occasional flame flickered and here and there a wisp of

smoke rose from the circular heap of ashes after the two braves, still obscenely exposed to the vacant stare of the woman, moved away from the fire toward her. There was nothing hurried about the actions of the Indians, which seemed to heighten the menace of their evil eagerness to take the woman whom they were certain of having at their mercy.

Adam Steele was equally deliberate as he eased the rifle from his boot and thumbed back the hammer to cock the action of this very special Colt Hartford revolving model. And then brought his left hand up from the saddlehorn, letting go of the reins, to grip the barrel as he pushed the stock against his shoulder and rested his cheek to the polished and fire-charred rosewood. Drew a bead on the broad, naked back of the Apache on the left – the one who was sliding a hunting knife from a sheath on his weapons belt. Intending to use the gun glinting blade not to slice through her bond, or to kill her. Instead, to cut the clothes from her sweating and trembling body, so that the second brave who was in process of unfastening his belt and removing his breechclout would be unimpeded as he came down to take her.

They were perhaps six feet from her when they veered to left and right, to go to either side of her. And she sucked in a great gulp of scorchingly hot air that acted unwittingly to provocatively emphasise the thrusting firmness of her upper body. In fact, the intake of breath was used to power an outburst of shrill and fast-spoken Spanish. Uttered not in the tone of a plea for release – instead was quite obviously a diatribe of invective. Which, whether they understood it or merely guessed at its meaning from the tenor in which it was delivered, drew further gusts of laughter from the Apaches.

But then she curtailed the tirade as she caught sight of the mounted man up on the ridge in the deep shade of the rock. And needed to do a double take to be sure she was not seeing a vision conjured up by her anguished mind. While for the stretched seconds of her sudden silence the Apaches who now were standing close to her head and between her splayed legs thought she had run out of breath or was suddenly paralysed by throat-constricting fear. Until she bellowed, the loudest yet:

'*Tirar, hombre! Tirar a matar! Haga el favor, senor! Madre de Dios*!'

The saliva of relief flooded into her throat and she choked on it. Had to spit it out before she could go on. While the brave with the knife stooped and made to cut open her shirt from the neckline. But saw something compelling in her staring eyes that forced him to look in the same direction – and to snarl a monosyllabic warning to his naked partner as he straightened up and whirled.

'Shoot them!' the woman shrieked. 'Kill them! Please, I beg of you!'

Relief had been displaced by misery as she was convinced the stranger had left his attack too late. For both the braves had swung around to face the horseman now – the one with the knife having dropped this so that he could draw an ancient Navy Model Colt from his weapons belt. While the naked Apache had snatched a long barrel Smith and Wesson Russian revolver from the belt he had been about to dispense with when the single word warning was spoken.

'*Cabron*!' the woman hissed through clenched and exposed teeth. And then the sneer formed by the line of her drawn back teeth became a smile when she saw the puff of smoke at the muzzle of the stranger's rifle. A smile which broadened as she raced her eyes along their sockets and she was in time to see, at the same instant she heard the report of the rifle shot, the small dark hole appear in the chest of the brave who stood at her head.

This brave took a staggering step backwards, with blood trickling from a hole at the side of his left nipple and a groan of anguish spilling out of his sagged-open mouth. Then he fell hard to his knees and folded forward, in such a way that the woman had to wrench her head to the side and jerk it up off the ground to avoid being smothered beneath the blood-run chest of the now dead Apache.

The second brave, totally naked except for his moccasins and single feathered headband, triggered a shot from his long barrel revolver just as the first one started to fall forward – had taken the time to bring up the Russian in a double-handed grip and steady his aim. The woman was concerned with evading the falling corpse when she heard what sounded like an echo off the hillside of the revolver shot. But then the dead man was sprawled full length on the ground and she was resting her head against his unfeeling hip – able to see the second Apache go down. Killed by another heart shot against the impact of which he struggled to stand upright and, as a result, toppled like a felled tree, his body and limbs not becoming lax until his brain ceased to function when his fall was almost complete. He weighed heavily in an arched back attitude over her lower right leg and foot. She watched in horrified fascination as his former extended erection softened and withered.

Up on the ridge beside the outcrop of weathered sandstone, Adam Steele swung quickly down from his saddle. He still held his rifle around the frame with one hand. On his face was an expression of dark anger that found outlet in a snarled obscenity. This as he got both feet on the ground at the moment the mare lurched to the side, away from him. And for several moments leaned against the sheer face of the rock in a desperate attempt to remain upright. While in her bulging brown eyes there was an eloquent plea to the man. That she was doing her best to stay on her feet because this is what she thought was expected of her – but she wanted badly to sprawl out on her side. Then the blood that had entered her punctured lung showed on her teeth and lips, a deeper shade of crimson than that which oozed from the wound in back of her first rib on the left side.

'You were the best, girl,' the Virginian said softly, his accent still as strongly of the South as it was the day, long ago, when he was forced to leave the state of his birth.

And his expression was for a short time one of compassionate understanding as he took deliberate aim at the head of the dying horse, to squeeze the trigger and blast a bullet at point blank range into the brain of the animal. To kill her instantly on her feet, so that she felt nothing physically nor emotionally as she dropped heavily to the ground at the foot of the outcrop.

'*Senor*!' the woman called, pain in her voice, from the base of the slope. 'I am grateful to you for what you have done already. All I ask of you now is that you set me free so that I may move away from these heathen savages!'

There was little blood from the head wound. But a great deal was spilled from the animal's mouth when she hit the ground and the impact had a pumping effect as her holed lung was compressed. The vital organ punctured by a million to one chance shot that the Virginian should not have given the Apache the time to fire.

'*Senor*? You hear me? You understand? *Usted comprender*?'

During both periods she shouted up the slope to him and, throughout the utter silence in between, Adam Steele stood absolutely still: the rifle canted to his left shoulder, his face altering in expression from compassion through regret, to bitter anger and finally to impassiveness. And only when he had run the gamut of these emotions to reach ice coolness did he turn from the waist to look away from the dead mare and down at the woman who leaned against one dead Apache and was partially underneath another Indian.

'Understand English, lady!' he called to her. 'And I heard you! Be with you when I'm through up here!'

He leaned the rifle against the outcrop and stooped beside the carcase. There was a split in the outside seam of his right pants leg between knee and shin, and this gaped when he bent his leg, so that he was able to insert a hand and draw a knife from a boot sheath. He used the knife to cut free one of his saddlebags. Then replaced the knife and unfastened the ties that had kept his bedroll in place while he rose. He was also able to salvage the reins and the blood-stained bridle and bit. The saddle and the other bag and both canteens were trapped beneath the immovable dead weight of the carcase.

'I do not wish to sound ungrateful after what you have done for me, *senor*!' the woman called, irritably impatient, as Steele reached for his rifle and turned to move away from the horse. 'But every second I am forced to remain here with these dead savages seems to last an hour!'

'I'm through now,' he answered and now she looked up at him again, after keeping her eyes tightly closed for a long time. And smiled her relief that he was starting down the steep slope.

'Please hurry!' she shouted, suddenly distressed again. 'Oh . . . *Madre de Dios*! It is starting, *senor! Mi regla*!' Her tone became shriller and she struggled against her bonds and the dead Indian who draped one of her legs – like she felt there was a chance she could wrench herself free by brute force. She swung her head from side to side. Then became limp, exhausted in defeat, the back of her head toward the Virginian who continued to pick his way carefully down the treacherous slope. 'It is too late,' she said miserably. 'It has started now. How do you say it . . . my period has come.'

'It's that kind of a day for you, I reckon, lady,' Steele answered evenly. 'Just one bloody thing after another.'

CHAPTER TWO

THE MEXICAN woman kept her head turned away from the Virginian as he approached her. And vented a gasp when the dead Apache who had fallen across her leg was dragged clear. Then she began to weep softly as Steele drew the knife from the boot sheath again and cut the ropes that held her wrists and ankles to the stakes.

He said nothing as he freed her, his attention constantly focused on the task that occupied him. Then, as he rose from crouching beside her he offered:

'There you go, lady. You need anything from me to do what you have to?'

'*Senor*, I would very much like to have privacy,' she answered, struggling to quell her tears.

'You have it,' he told her and moved to where he had set down what he had salvaged from the dead horse. Stood in an easy attitude beside the heap of gear, gazing south from the camp at the base of the rise: his back toward the woman and everything she needed. And for a long time all that disturbed the silence of the desert was the occasional suppressed sob from the woman as she continued to lay where she had been a captive: needing to recover some kind of composure before she felt able to move.

But when she was at length able to will herself to rise from the ground, she went quickly about her business – at the waterhole and then close to the burros hobbled beside the cottonwood. No longer weeping, but breathing noisily as if from hard exertion. And now and then she uttered a groan of anguish. This while Adam Steele stood stoically on the fringe of the camp, as unmoving and as silent as the natural features of the desert over which he gazed.

He was aware that the woman often looked toward him and was conscious of the change that came over her as time went by – that at first she was nervous he might turn around too early and discover her in some embarrassing chore, but soon she began to eye him in an appraising manner and was quite obviously curious about him.

What she saw was a man who, at first glance, looked not at all capable of carrying out the rescue that he had only minutes ago undertaken. He was about forty years of age and stood in the region of five and a half feet tall. His build was slight and he was not strikingly handsome. His clothing looked to have been made in a rush from garments originally intended to fit a much bigger man.

'*Gracias, senor,*' she said. 'I am all finished now.'

He stooped to pick up his gear before he turned to face her and replied: 'I'll need to have one of the burros to replace my horse.'

She was standing at the side of the waterhole, wearing the same black shirt but a different pair of pants. She had washed her face and was now finger combing her hair. The wan smile she had started to build was abruptly wiped out by the coldness of his tone and the matching grimness of his expression. And as he moved around the other side of the waterhole from where she stood to get the animals, she was struck by how wrong she had been to consider that he had reacted out of character in the way he dealt with the Apache braves.

She had been correct about his age and his height. But his build was lean rather than slight and he had considerable strength compacted in his body. He was not overly good looking because there was a mark of cruelty, difficult to define, in his face. A face of regular features with coal black eyes and a skin that was darkly stained by exposure to the elements and patterned with countless lines. His hair was almost entirely grey and only in the long sideburns that reached almost to his jawline was there an occasional trace of the red it once had been. He looked not to have shaved for two or three days, but usually was clean-shaven.

He was dressed in an old and stained black Stetson, a once white shirt, grey pants and black riding boots without spurs. He had no coat nor vest and neither did he wear a gunbelt: and as she watched him load his gear on to one of the burros, the woman vented a grunt of discovery.

'You say something, lady?' Steele asked.

'My name, it is Rosa Canales.'

'Adam Steele. It's nice to know you.'

'You must realise how glad I am to know you, *Senor* Steele.'

He looked appraisingly at her now, as he completed loading the burro by thrusting his rifle into his bedroll. And saw that his first impression of her build had been correct – she was perhaps an inch taller than he was and had a fine figure. And a firm one, as befitted a woman who – now that she had cleaned the dirt from her face – he could see was in her early twenties. Both the tone of her skin and the shape of her features revealed her Hispanic bloodline. In different circumstances she would come close to being beautiful, Steele guessed. This afternoon, the effects of her recent ordeal made her look drained and even haggard.

'I reckon so.'

'I have not even expressed my thanks for setting me free.'

'It was nothing.'

'To me it was everything, *Senor* Steele. It is words that are nothing after such a thing has been done. But they are all I can offer for now. If you will help me further, though, I can promise you a large reward.'

'The burro is fine, Miss Canales.'

She had started to look more at ease during the exchange. But now she became strained by nervous tension again and there was misery in her voice when she said: 'Of course, *senor*. You have your own business to attend to.'

She nodded her head slowly as she spoke and then Steele shook his head when he answered:

'Whatever my business is, it can wait until I take you some place you'll be safe, Miss Canales. All I said is that I don't want anything for my trouble except the burro.'

He crouched to unfasten the hobbles on the forelegs of both animals. Then swung easily up into the saddle of the one laden with his gear.

'Some place? You have such a place in mind, *Senor* Steele?'

'I'm a stranger here. I reckoned you weren't and so – '

She strode fast from the waterhole to halt in front of the mounted Virginian. For a moment seemed not to know how to get started on what she needed to say, but then took a deep breath and spoke in a rush.

'*Senor*, I know that it does not look to be so, but I am a very rich woman. But the appearances, they can be very deceptive, no? As with you. Which I decide after watching you for a long time. My father, he is Don Benito Canales of De Raza Hacienda which is in Chihuahua, Mexico. And if you will escort me back to my home my father will richly reward you.'

Her dark eyes expressed a tacitly eloquent plea that he should agree to do as she asked.

'Where abouts in Chihuahua, Miss Canales?' Steele asked.

'In the northern part, *senor*,' she replied eagerly. 'Close to the Rio Bravo. The Rio Grande is how you Americans call it. Some miles south of Ciudad Juerez, which is just across the border from El Paso in the state of Texas.'

She was like an over excited child, on tenterhooks while she waited for Steele to consider what she had told him: while her mind raced to search for further inducements to him. Then, when he gave a nod, she vented a gust of relieved laughter as she lunged forward and clambered up astride the other burro – as childlike in this as she had been while she waited for his response.

'You live back that way,' Steele told her with a jerk of his thumb to indicate the rise with the outcrop and dead horse on its ridge. Then he nodded toward the south, along the line of sign left by the two Apaches and their prisoner. 'But they brought you from that way.'

The woman glanced across at the dead braves flanking the area where she had been staked out and was once more weak with remembered horror as she shuddered. Then she dragged her gaze back to the Virginian. Said:

'I do not know what is to the far side of this hill, *senor.* To the south is a trail which I was riding when the savages took me. It is a trail that goes all the way to El Paso. Not an easy trail, perhaps, but I think it is maybe easier to ride than across the country from here.' She looked up the steep slope and shrugged. 'You came from there, though. Perhaps you know – '

'South to the trail, Miss Canales. I've come from a lot of places. Right now from the north. Wherever a man's coming from or going to, a trail makes the travelling easier.'

He heeled his burro forward and the woman was quick to start her mount and move the animal up alongside the other one – as if she was afraid to be too far away from her rescuer. And when they were riding side by side, she seemed to need to take time to control her emotions and organise her thinking again. Showing that she had consciously to make the effort, while Adam Steele remained in what to the woman looked to be a comfortable silence.

'In the north, you had some trouble, *senor*?' she said when the camp beside the waterhole was perhaps a half mile behind them.

'Some,' he allowed.

'More than that, I think?'

'Less than you were in, Miss Canales.'

'We have far to go, *senor.* Why do you not call me Rosa? And I may call you Adam, perhaps?'

The Virginian shrugged.

'I am a young woman away from her home and family for the first time. Not familiar with what is necessary to avoid such a thing happening to me. But you, *senor* . . . Adam, you dealt with my position in the manner of a man who has . . . who has had much experience of such things.'

'Rosa?'

His tone added the query and she shot a sidelong glance at him.

'Adam?'

'You want to get to the point about me that's bothering you?'

She was perplexed for a moment – not confused by what he said, but instead unsure of how to express herself. Until she shrugged and told him simply: 'You do not look to be the kind of man who is capable of doing as you did. Do you understand what I say?'

Steele nodded and looked down at himself. Then showed a fleeting smile that was almost boyish as he growled: 'The burro about puts the finishing touch, uh?'

'I am sorry your horse is dead, Adam.'

'It was the mare's bad luck. On two counts. That I was riding her and I had to have the Indians facing me before I shot them. And that she took the bullet that was meant for me – and a thousand other times would have gone wide.'

When he spoke of the bullet being aimed to hit him, he raised his left hand and absently massaged an area of his upper right chest – as if he had a dull ache there. And, before he lowered his hand, he looked at it as if he expected to see something on it. For the few seconds it took for this to happen, he was lost in remembered events and was unaware that the Mexican woman was speaking to him until she raised her voice to say:

'Adam?'

'Yes?'

'I said that if you do not wish to discuss your affairs, I understand.'

'That's good, Rosa,' he told her, and knew that she was irritated with herself for allowing him an opportunity she had obviously not expected him to take.

It had happened up in the timbered country of northern California that he took the bullet in the upper right side of his chest after he had got himself tied up with a half-breed Indian. Half Apache, coincidentally. He had done a lot of riding with the bullet deep inside him, mortifying the flesh around it. But death by the hanging rope had been the main threat at the start. The lynch rope in a squalid mining town. Which he escaped, only to run the risk of dying from a combination of exposure and gangrene before he was discovered in the hollow that could well have been his final resting place. But those who found him and nursed him back along the road to health unwittingly delivered him into the hands of a close knit community where he was in danger of being tried for murder by due process of law and, if found guilty, hanged in the name of justice.

It was from this series of close calls with death that he had been riding when he smelled the brushwood smoke and followed his horse to the camp where Rosa Canales was in imminent danger of being used and abused by the Apache braves. The horse had been his. And the saddle and accoutrements, too. They were his own boots. And knife and rifle. All else had been taken from and off him after he was found in the hollow.

Which was little enough when compared with what this man had had taken from him many years earlier. For Adam Steele had been born the only son of one of the richest plantation owners in the state of Virginia, and enjoyed the privileges of wealth and position as he grew to young manhood, working to learn all there was to know about the business he had no reason to expect he would not one day inherit. But then came the brutal War Between the States which, as it did in many instances, opened a rift between the Steele father and son. For Adam left home to fight for the

Confederacy while Ben gave covert assistance to the Union.

For the four years of bloody conflict, Adam Steele rode as a cavalry lieutenant and underwent many changes of attitude toward his father. And when the uneasy peace came, both men were unscathed physically and felt emotionally prepared to forget their differences and start anew. But it was not to be. Ben Steele died on the same night as Abraham Lincoln. In the same city and just as wastefully – was lynched from a beam in a bar room as part of a conspiracy by fanatics not willing to accept defeat for the Southern Cause.

On that same night, Adam Steele killed for the first time without the protection of a uniform: before he took the body of his father home to bury. But home no longer existed, except in terms of acres of land scorched by the burning of the cotton and tobacco crops, with – at the centre – the blackened skeleton of the big house that had also been put to the torch.

All that was saved was the Colt Hartford rifle with the engraved gold plate screwed to the right side of the rosewood stock, the inscription reading: *To Benjamin P. Steele, with gratitude – Abraham Lincoln.* After he buried the corpse of his father, Adam Steele set off with this rifle to track down and kill every man who had a hand in the lynching. But he was too single-minded in his determination to exact vengeance: and the innocent as well as the guilty died during the opening days of the violent peace.

In war, it is expected and accepted that the innocent suffer sometimes, but in times of peace the law must be upheld. And so it was that Adam Steele became wanted for murder and could not return to claim what remained of his birthright and build upon it some semblance of what it once had been. Instead, he was forced to head west beyond the frontier, where the only law that mattered was that which dictated what man must do to survive. There were very many variations of this law, but the basic premise was that the fittest man survived at the expense of those who fell short – fitness in a physical sense not often a primary requirement.

Since the first violent trail had come to an end with the death of the men who lynched Ben Steele – and the cold blooded murder of the deputy sheriff who had been Adam Steele's best friend – the exiled Virginian had travelled countless miles in search of the unattainable and for the first few years had been unwilling to admit that he was clutching at straws. Back in those days it had been his ambition to find some spot west of the Mississippi where he might put down fresh roots and create something akin to his pre-war life in Virginia. And while he searched he attempted as opportunity allowed to maintain certain of the standards that had been effortlessly taken for granted during his early years.

He dressed as elegantly as money allowed, in city style apparel that often got him called a dude. He sacrificed to afford good food when the occasion offered. He was very fastidious about bathing and shaving even under the most primitive of conditions. And the women he went with had to match up to the mark where he considered they became ladies.

But that period of sustained effort to maintain former standards had ended long ago: when he was finally forced to face up to the facts of his life in the wake of losing everything that at one time he thought had made it worth living. Realised he was destined to be a rootless drifter who had to take what he needed as it became available, to compromise if it did not measure up to his precise requirements – and be prepared to lose it to the dictates of a compassionless fate.

'Adam?' Rosa Canales said softly and rather tentatively, as if she was nervous about breaking the lengthy silence – anxious about how he would respond to having his concentration disturbed.

'Something, Rosa?' the Virginian replied evenly, not so deeply immersed in past events as before. And his dark eyes when they glanced at her held an expression of mild interest in what she had it in mind to say. In much the same way as he had been maintaining a constant survey over their surroundings as they trekked southward astride the slow moving burros.

'You and I, we are much alike, I think.'

'How so?' he countered as he took up his apparently casual watch in every direction again – his gaze merely raking over her as a component part of what lay to the west. She and her mount the only living things seen to move on his right. While to the north, more than a mile behind them by now, a once high flying bird spiralled downward and glided gracefully to a precise landing. Showed itself definitely to be a buzzard rather than an eagle as it began to feast ravenously on the naked and near naked corpses of the two Apaches.

'I have told you of my father and his wealth. And you see me like this.' She looked down at herself and then gestured with both hands to stress dismay with her dirty and dishevelled appearance. 'I think you, too, have known better times, Adam.'

'Better and worse, Rosa. But a man has to take the rough with the smooth, I reckon.' He smiled after voicing the trite old saw which he had not used in a very long time – maybe not since the rough times had begun to outnumber the smooth?

He did not elaborate and was again at ease with the silence which she found taxing as they rode across terrain that he seemed to think a deal more interesting than she was. And sometimes, he knew, she came close to venting an ill-tempered outburst against his constraint. But always she swallowed her irritation with him as she recalled what she owed him: or at least he assumed this was the reason why she took such obvious pains to curb her emotions.

Until she began to weep.

At first, he was unaware of this – he thought that the hand passes she made across her cheeks were to wipe off beads of sweat or to wave off the flies that were beginning to be bothersome as the warmth of the afternoon declined at the approach of evening. But then, by accident or womanly design, her face was not quite averted when he glanced in her direction and he saw the fading light of the sinking sun glinting against the salt wetness of her dark eyes.

'You have another problem, Rosa?' he asked then, eyeing her levelly.

She snapped her head to the side to hide her face, like she was ashamed to be seen weeping. And answered morosely: 'It does not matter.'

'Something we have to stop for? We can hold up for awhile here. Or make night camp in that grove of cottonwoods over by those rocks if you want?'

He nodded toward the possible campsite some half a mile ahead of them. Where the long hill that had always been to their left since they left the waterhole, gradually losing height, finally came to an end at an area of scattered boulders and scree fringed by some ragged timber.

'It is nothing. I am being foolish. I can go on for as long as you require.'

'Just to the cottonwoods will be fine for today.'

And the place he had picked out from a distance was where they made camp. Rosa Canales dry eyed as they approached the cottonwoods and then eager to do her share of the chores in gathering fuel, building the fire, preparing the food and cooking it. And she talked a great deal while she took care of all this and the Virginian attended to the animals' needs after he had relieved them of their saddles and other paraphernalia – then sat with his back against the base of a tree and watched her. While the light of the sun diminished, but night's darkness was kept at bay from the grove by the flickering flames of the fire. That were needed, soon, to warm the man and the woman who moved closer to the fire as the desert's night coldness began to make itself felt.

Her talk was of inconsequentials – started with a recounting of a hunting and camping expedition her father had taken her on when she was a child. Which memory triggered off many other recollections of happy times on and around De Raza Hacienda. Of her father teaching her to ride, of birthday parties at which she was showered with gifts, of trips to cities on both sides of the border.

In the telling of her stories she was childlike again. And needed no encouragement from her listener beyond his attention. Which he gave her, seemingly undivided – she unaware that he was listening with just half an ear. In the darkness of night searched out alien and perhaps menacing sounds in back of her voice and the crackle of the fire. Just as by day he relied primarily upon his eyes to spot the first sign of potential danger.

Then she was through, just a minute or so after they had finished eating their meal of chili and were drinking coffee. And now she appeared to be as comfortable without words as he had always showed himself to be. Until he broke the silence after he emptied his coffee cup.

'The feller who gave you all those good times, Rosa? He the same Don Benito Canales who you said would pay me for taking you home?'

'Of course,' she replied quickly, bewildered by the question.

'Way you've told it, nothing worth the telling happened to you after you were about sixteen. Thought that maybe he had gone away or died or – '

'I tell you of when I was a young girl, Adam,' she cut in on him and there was abruptly a tone of strain in her voice again. 'When a girl becomes a woman, it is not always only within herself that there are changes. Around her it is not as it always was. You understand this? It is the same for *los jovenes* become *los hombres*, no? When boys change into men?'

'Maybe,' Steele allowed. 'But it's easier. On the whole, young fellers are better able to take care of themselves if they take it into their heads to run away from home.'

'Who said I have run away?' she snapped.

Steele shrugged, and set his empty cup down beside his plate. 'Not you, Rosa,' he told her evenly as he wrapped a blanket around himself and stretched out on the ground – head resting on a burro saddle and left hand fisted around the frame of the Colt Hartford. 'And it's my belief you haven't lied to me yet.'

'Why should I lie to you, Adam?' she protested.

'I don't know, Rosa. I do know that from here to home is a long way. But I wasn't going any place in particular. For no pay but with nobody to worry about except myself.'

'I think perhaps you never concern yourself with anybody else, Adam.'

He had put his hat over his face to blot out fire, moon and star light. But could hear her gathering up the dirty dishes and moving about the camp as she spoke.

'The better the pay, the more I'm concerned about the work I'm doing.'

'How does five thousand dollars sound to you, Adam?' she posed with a trace of scorn in her voice.

'Like a matter of great concern.'

CHAPTER THREE

ADAM STEELE slept shallowly but awoke rested and refreshed with the first grey light of the new day. Which was how it had been for many days now – a sign that he was fully recovered from at least one aspect of the bullet wound and its poisonous after-effects.

For a long time before he began to become aware that he was on the way to recovery, it had not been that way at all. During that period, he reflected upon how as he re-kindled the fire and started coffee to boiling, when Julia French had taken care of him. A time when he was completely oblivious to all that was happening around him while he slept close to unconsciousness and when, even when he was awake, he relied on the woman to do so much for him. Others had helped, not least two precocious children, but his memory of the rest was blurred by the vividness of the images of the bespectacled Julia.

She it was who had made for him, from the garments of another man, the clothing he wore now. To replace the once dudish garb that was ruined after his gruelling experience of being shot and then almost hanged. And she it was who had given him most help to escape death again in a place where he might well have been able to sink new roots had he been in a different frame of mind . . . or had Julia been of a mind to try to change his viewpoint.

But the time or the circumstances or the woman had not been right and so he had left her up in a rich valley of Six Rivers County. To head south for no other reason than the going in that direction was easiest. Taking his time to put the miles behind him and to get back his health. Waiting for fresh trouble to erupt around him and not entirely sure he would be able to handle it until he could remain alert without effort during the waking hours and sleep like an animal even when exhausted.

And that fresh trouble had come when he found the Apaches about to rape this other woman whom he now stood over, on the point of waking. The Indians, they had been dealt with easily. But this Hispanically beautiful young woman who he was certain was what she claimed to be – the daughter of a wealthy father – could well prove to cost him more than two bullets and a good horse: so that the five thousand dollars she had spoken of might not be adequate pay for the job he had agreed to accept.

He touched her on the blanket-draped and pants-covered rump with the toe of a booted foot and she came awake with a choked scream and an expression of terror. Which did not surprise him, since she had been sleeping with a look of strain distorting her face and often cried out softly between short periods of irregular breathing.

'There you go, Rosa,' he said evenly, stooping to hand her a cup of coffee. 'Sun's up and so should you be, if you really are eager to get home.'

'*Quisiera* . . . ' she began after blinking her dark eyes several times, and fisting the grit of sleep from them. Then she sat up, knees tucked to her conical breasts and back arched, and held out both hands to accept the coffee. '*Muchas gracias.* I am sorry, *senor* . . . Adam. It is never good for me in the early morning. Last night I had bad dreams. I did not know where I was when you woke me. I thought the two savages . . . '

She began to sip at the coffee, grateful for its reviving effect and relishing its taste.

'I can understand how that might be, Rosa,' the Virginian said as he set down his cup for the coffee to cool while he started to prepare the burros for leaving. 'But now you've had a full night's sleep and you know who I am and that I made sure those particular Apaches won't bother you again.'

She kept nodding as he spoke. Then: '*Si*, Adam. Yes, I am feeling much better this morning. Yesterday, it was as if you were part of the same *horroroso* – the same horrible – thing that happened to me with the Indians. I am so sorry.'

'Nothing was lost.'

'I wanted somebody to talk to. There was just you. A man like you, he has no interest in what a frightened woman has to say – just for the sake of talking. I kept becoming angry while we travelled here and I think you know this. But when we come to this place, you are patient and listen.'

Steele cinched the second saddle to the second burro and urged: 'Soon as you're through with the blanket and cup, we can get started.'

He picked up his own cup and finished its contents in two swallows. She hurried to finish her coffee, then gave her blanket to him to stow while she attempted to clean the cups.

'I must attend to myself,' she said, discomfited and with her head hung down.

'You're not the first woman I've ever come across, Rosa,' Steele assured her. 'And once I was even married for awhile – or thought I was.'

'*Gracias*,' she said in relief and moved quickly into the grove of cottonwoods. And assured him when she re-emerged a few minutes later: 'I was as quick as I could be.'

'Reckon you weren't in any condition to take notice of the country the Apaches hauled you across?' the Virginian asked when she had mounted her burro.

From the way he looked about, the woman grasped the point of his question and shook her head. 'I can recognise none of this, Adam. The savages forced me to walk behind the animals and sometimes they ride fast so that I cannot keep up and am dragged. But they capture me at my camp in the early morning and leave with me right away. Where you find me is the first place they stop. So it is a long way from the trail. I think perhaps they take me so far because they are afraid they will be followed and caught.'

'Reckon that's right,' Steele agreed and led the way clear of the morning shade of the cottonwoods, into the glare of the fully risen sun that already gave promise of the high heat it would shed later in the day.

The sign left by the Apache-burdened burros and the Mexican woman captive on the trek northwards was still visible across a landscape that was now a flat scrub desert for almost as far as the eye could see to the east and the west. While to the north were the Marias and in the distant south was another range of low and jagged-topped hills.

'There, perhaps,' the woman said at length, raising a faintly shaking arm to point to the south. 'I was camped in hill country when they captured me. I was so frightened after that I cannot say . . . ' She shrugged her slender shoulders and chewed the inside of a cheek. 'But perhaps it was in those hills that the trail I was following ran.'

'Runs to where, Rosa?'

'Where nearby, I do not know, Adam. It was to the city of San Francisco that I was going when I set out from home.'

'Did you pass through any place that was more than a church, a saloon and a couple of houses not too far back along the trail?'

'Phoenix in Arizona Territory was the last place like that, Adam. Where I had to sell the wagon to buy supplies. And was cheated in the deal on the burros, I think. But, as you said, it is easier for young men than for young women.'

'Phoenix was way back, I reckon?'

She nodded, grim faced as she recalled unpleasant memories. 'Five days on the burros from there to the Colorado River where this state of California has border with Territory of Arizona, Adam.'

'There were some smaller places in between?'

'Yes. Not many. You have reason for asking, I am sure?' She looked and sounded a little worried.

'We'll need to get supplies at one of the small towns, Rosa,' he answered absently. 'I guess I'll have to wait until we reach Phoenix before I can get some decent clothes.'

She was unable to suppress a short laugh of relief that his interrogation concerned with communities along the trail had a motive that did not affect her. When he directed a sidelong look at the woman, though, she boasted:

'I knew I was right about you and I being alike in some ways, Adam! And in other ways, not at all similar.'

'Reckon it would be stupid to argue with that,' the Virginian answered sardonically.

Rosa Canales vented a groan of self-disgust now, annoyed at how badly she had expressed herself. 'I mean that once times were good for you. Maybe you were rich, even. Familiar, as I have been, with the finer things of life.'

'Didn't I say that I was?'

'Not in so many words.'

'All right, Rosa. Once, a long time ago, I was rich and I reckon I've enjoyed most of the finer things in life that money can buy. But it ended, through no fault of my own, I like to think. And since it did the times haven't all been bad. There have been as many ups as there have been downs, maybe. And a lot of those ups could not have been bought for money.'

'Adam, I – '

'You asked, and I might as well get said everything I intend to on the subject,' he interrupted her interruption, his tone even while she appeared anxious that her questions had irritated him. 'Since I haven't been rich, I've moved around a lot, Rosa. And have become what I am without having to try too hard. Which maybe means I haven't changed too much from what I used to be. But it sure seems to me that nothing much stays the same for long. Unless I make the effort. This rifle was all my father left me.' He draped a hand briefly over the stock of the Colt Hartford jutting out of the bedroll strapped to the saddle behind him. 'And right now it's all I have left that's been constantly with me while so much else has been changing.

'Unless you count the rig I carry my knife in. But I class that as part of my clothing, Rosa. The knife itself isn't the one I started out with. And most clothes wear out. I've changed them a dozen times or maybe more. Except for the gloves, which were sure in sore need of replacement. And the kerchief that wasn't what it seemed – could be more deadly than the rifle or the knife at real close range. I'll maybe have a new one made up for me. And certainly I'll buy a fresh pair of buckskin gloves when I go shopping for a suit and all the trimmings.'

While he spoke in his soft and easy Virginian drawl, Adam Steele maintained his deceptively casual surveillance over the sun-parched desert towards horizons closed in by heat haze. But there was a certain quality of vagueness in the man's attitude – like he was lost in deep reflection of secret doubts and was perhaps not aware he was speaking aloud his thoughts. And so, worried again about angering the impassive-faced man riding at her side, the Mexican woman this time made no attempt at a comment.

Then, when Steele glimpsed the look of concern on her attractive face, he vented a short laugh and urged: 'Hey, you can tell now why I don't talk so much, Rosa?'

'Adam?'

'Because when I do, I talk a lot of cra . . . of nonsense.'

'I do not think this, Adam,' she assured him earnestly. 'I think what you have said is that in a world, in a life, where there is much change all the time, a person feels the need of some kind of permanence. And I think you laugh at this because you are a little ashamed to have such a need. But it is not wrong. You require little enough. The weapons to protect yourself with and the fine clothing from inside of which you find it better to face the world and the people in it?'

For perhaps a full two seconds he held the quizzical look in her dark eyes with a steady gaze from his own of a similar hue. And she was not at all anxious about his temperament now. Then he nodded shortly and shifted his attention away from her to take up his survey of their glaringly bright, seemingly empty of life surroundings again. And allowed:

'Maybe you're right, Rosa.'

'Most of us need much more, Adam,' she augmented in the same sober tone and wearing the same solemn expression. 'A home to escape to, many more possessions than you have, an absorbing interest, a family, friends, somebody who is more than a friend . . . '

She let the sentence hang in the hot air and Steele did not accept the invitation to end the pause until after he had done a double take into the shimmering distance ahead. Then offered:

'A friend of that kind the reason you left home, Rosa?'

'*Si*! Yes!' She was much more eager to talk about her recent past than the Virginian had been to reveal the reason for his discontent. But she made an effort to curb her enthusiasm before she explained: 'I have had many suitors, Adam. Few of them serious and even fewer that I was able to take seriously. Until I fall in love with Esteban Chevez and he returns my love. But he is just a *vaquero* for my father on De Raza Hacienda, Adam. A poor man who anyway is not popular with my father. Esteban and I, we know it is useless to go to my father for his blessing. So we make plans to run away. But these are discovered by the spies of my father. Esteban, he is badly beaten and told that if ever he comes back to the hacienda again, he will be killed. I leave the hacienda because of this bad business, Adam. With some hope of finding Esteban, perhaps. Or perhaps not. But I made my way toward the city of San Francisco because it is of this place that Esteban and I spoke often.'

'We didn't sign any contract or even shake hands on a deal, Rosa.'

'I do not understand, Adam?'

'You're older than twenty-one, I reckon?'

'*Si.*' She remained puzzled.

'So you have the legal right to go wherever you like and do whatever you want. And if you want to change your mind again and go to San Francisco instead of back home, I'm not about to hold you to what you said you wanted while you were still getting over what the Apaches – '

She began to shake her head emphatically and then was unable to curb her impatience until he was finished. Broke in on him:

'No, Adam! It is why I have said you and I have much that is common between us. I should not be out here like this. It was a mistake and I wish now to be back at home where I belong. *Estar como gallina en corral ajeno*, is how we say I am in my language. Like the fish . . . '

'Fish out of water, Rosa.'

'*Si*,' she agreed with another eager nod. 'Me through my own stupidity, I admit. You not so, I am sure. We are not alike at all in this respect, I think. You are not at all stupid, Adam. And if you are caused the inconvenience by the stupidity of others, you are well able to overcome this by your own efforts. While I owe my honour and perhaps my life to you. And would give little for my chance of returning safely home unless you remain with me?'

She had been staring down at her hands which held the reins while she spoke and only looked up and to the side after she had implied the plea. And this time she saw the intensity of his gaze directed toward the heat-hazed hills in the forward distance.

'Something is the matter, Adam?' she asked, anxiety intruding a briefly unswallowable lump in her throat.

'Reckon there's a man on a horse in that high ground, Rosa. Which doesn't have to mean something is wrong.'

He was again looking elsewhere, but she stared fixedly ahead.

'A savage?'

'Too far off to tell.'

She jutted out a lower lip to direct a draught of cooling air over her sweat-beaded face. Then she unhooked a canteen and took a deep swallow of water. Next sighed and smiled wanly before she assured herself: 'But I think I have no need to worry, Adam. Before, I was alone and not convinced I was truly doing what I wanted. Now I have you to protect me and I am certain that to get back home is all I want. I thank you for listening to me, Adam. *Muchas gracias.*'

'It's maybe been repaid with interest, Rosa. Couple of things, though?'

'*Si*? Yes?'

'When we get closer to where you live, there's no chance you're going to have another change of mind?'

An emphatic shake of her head now, the long and jet black hair swinging and rustling. 'No, Adam. Even more I am not like you. Before I was taken by the savages and thought it was the end or perhaps worse than the end for me, I had begun to regret my decision to leave. I know I need more than you do to feel happy.'

'And your father will pay five thousand dollars to have you back home?'

'I can offer you nothing more than my word that he will pay,' she answered gravely. 'I think if you will ask for ten times this much, he will pay. When he is told from what you saved me. Five thousand dollars seemed like fair payment. Less would be *tacana* . . . how is it you say – stingy. For me to promise more when I made the offer – perhaps it would not have sounded possible my father was rich enough. But you will see, Adam. When we reach De Raza Hacienda, you will see the extent of the wealth of Don Benito Canales and I will be happy for you to ask for however much you think is reasonable and I am worth. And my father will be most happy to pay you.'

'Grateful to you, Rosa. But we agreed on five thousand.'

She sighed, then smiled. 'That is good, Adam. Like the

Canales family, you have honour. A deal made is a deal sealed, no?'

'Right, Rosa,' the Virginian agreed, and allowed his uncommunicative gaze to linger just a little longer than usual on the woman as he raked his eyes over the backdrop to her. 'Provided you're the only part of it that's stacked.'

CHAPTER FOUR

ROSA CANALES spoke excellent English, but her well-educated knowledge of the foreign language did not extend to the subleties of this *double-entendre*. Just for a moment or so, she appeared on the point of asking him to explain what he meant but then was quietly content to let the matter rest – fully satisfied with the outcome of the exchange. Sure he trusted her to be telling the truth and convinced that he truly was a man of his word.

This was how Adam Steele judged her attitude, anyway, as they rode slowly over the day old sign toward the line of hills: the fringes of which were no longer hazed by wet looking heat shimmer. The woman patently as comfortable with the lack of conversation as was he for almost an hour. When she opened the talk again, but on the safe subject of her happy home life before she was of an age to attract suitors. Talk to which the Virginian was required to contribute just an occasional word or so – even a grunt. And when she began to question him, it was also on areas of his past and his philosophies to which he could not object.

It was much easier now to avoid being distracted from his surveillance – with just her sexual attractiveness to contend with – and he saw, at the earliest it showed, the sign which had been left on the desert floor by the horse of the lone rider he had glimpsed twice at a distance. They were perhaps a mile and a half away from the base of the first hill when he spotted where the horse had been ridden out toward them and turned to backtrack when the man in the saddle noticed the Virginian and the Mexican woman on the burros.

The horse was shod, so was not an Indian pony.

Rosa gave no indication that she had seen the sign, but soon after she and Steele began to ride their mounts over the hoofprints that were a lot fresher than those made a day before by the burros, the woman became noticeably more tense. She spoke faster, sometimes softly and sometimes with a shrill tone of voice. If she asked questions, she allowed no time for a reply before changing the subject. She no longer even glanced at him and instead stared fixedly ahead. Her attention focused upon the fold between the two low hills through which both sets of signs led.

'Getting close now?' Steele cut in on what she was prattling.

'*Que*?'

'You remember this place, Rosa?'

'*Oh, si.*' She swallowed hard and looked at him and away again quickly, pressing a splayed hand across the shirt-contoured slopes of her upper breasts. 'Just beyond these hills, Adam, was where I camped for the night. At the side of the trail. It is where the savages were waiting when I awoke.'

She was almost as distressed now as she had been in the wake of his killing of the Apaches back at the waterhole. And only if he had doubted the authenticity of her emotions then could he have suspected her now. But why should he even consider for a second she might be shamming? He suppressed the question almost before he was through asking it of himself. And silence hung between the woman and him as they rode the curving course between the two hills – to reach the spot where there was proof positive of everything Rosa Canales had told him about her capture by the Apaches.

Beyond the desert facing slopes of the hills which were rocky, sandy and only sparsely featured with patches of brown grass and clumps of dust coloured brush, the terrain was less harsh. The hills, and some others to either side, comprised the northern flank of an east to west valley with a great many arroyos cutting down the steeper and higher grades of the southern flank. The creeks had been dry for most of the summer, but soon they would run with water again to replenish the underground stocks on which the unlush but fairly prolific vegetation of the valley had lived since the last big rains of spring.

The trail of which the Mexican woman had spoken ran along the precise centre of the valley; under-used and so not clearly defined for its entire length. Easier to see were the signs of Rosa's night camp and of the frightening activity that had taken place there.

She had made her camp just to the south of the trail under an almost sheer wall of sandstone, close by a stand of stunted ponderosa pine from which she had taken fuel for her fire. She had hobbled the burros to one side of the dwarf trees where they had fed themselves on some rabbitbrush. The Apaches had come down the southern slope of the valley, to the east of the cliff under which the woman was sleeping – doubtless homing in on the smoke of her dying fire. They had been on foot.

The man riding the shod horse had reached the former campsite on the trail from the east, his sign overlaying that left by the burros. After heading through the hills and out across the desert then backtracking to here, he had ridden up the south flank of the valley over the same route the braves had come down it. Now was either long gone or was in hiding. And in such a situation as this, Adam Steele was never able to trust his sixth sense for watching eyes.

The shadows of Steele and the woman, and of the burros they remained astride while he made his rapid appraisal of the scene and Rosa struggled to keep from trembling, were misshapenly truncated by the sun that was close to being directly overhead at this noon hour.

'Reckon you'd rather not rest up and eat here?' the Virginian queried.

She shook her head and now could not prevent a shudder – accompanied by a look of pleading. In response to which, he nodded, unhooked a canteen and drank a mouthful of the warm, mud-flavoured water. Said as he re-corked the canteen and heeled the burro forward:

'I'm not so hungry, anyway.'

'*Gracias* . . . thank you,' the woman managed to whisper. And seemed to want to add to this, but was afraid of a fresh bout of weeping.

And they rode in vocal silence for more than an hour, until the Virginian found a suitable stopping place. In the same valley as Rosa's former night camp but out of sight of it, and during the simple meal they had there in the shade of a single big cottonwood the tension of remembered terror gradually drained out of the woman. And she became talkative again as they started out on the afternoon ride. But either the high heat or the lack of responses from her audience of one – perhaps a combination of the two – eventually caused her to abandon the monologue. Without rancour or depression, though. And afterwards, she occasionally broke out into snatches of happy-sounding songs in her native language.

And was humming softly, like she had forgotten the words of the song, when Steele reined in his burro and spoke for the first time in perhaps two hours.

'Adam?' she asked, a little nervously, as she halted her mount.

'Sounds like moving water up ahead, Rosa.'

She cocked her head to the side to listen and then nodded that he was right. Looked about her, but was quite obviously unable to recall the area from when she last came through it.

'It all looks much the same as we have ridden through, Adam. And the shadows make so much difference.'

He nodded as they started along the trail again, their shadows distortedly elongated by the reddening sun that had already touched its leading edge to the high ground behind them.

'That much water has to be the Colorado, I reckon.'

'*Si*, Adam,' she agreed eagerly. 'That is the name. At the

last place I stop at in the Territory of Arizona, I am told that I must cross the *Rio* Colorado before the summer is over. Or perhaps I will not be able to cross in this part of the country.'

The river was making a rushing sound that was muted by distance – like the water was torrenting through a narrow gorge some way to the east.

'You have any trouble crossing it, Rosa?' Steele asked.

'No. There is a *vadera.*' She was perplexed for a moment as she searched for the English word she needed. 'Where the water is shallow. A ford, yes?'

Steele nodded as the sun set and the more subdued light of a half moon made an impression on the landscape. This at a point where the valley narrowed and forked – one arm angling to the north-east and the other to the south-east. The sound of the rushing water was funnelled from the north and the trail went toward the south. It was very dark in the moon-shadowed valley that had virtually become a gorge, with rock sides that got higher and sheerer as the ground started to slope toward the river.

The torrenting sound of the river forcing a way through another gorge was now totally muted by the intervening rocky terrain. And the noise of the human and animal intruders seemed over-emphasised in the otherwise complete silence. And Steele saw the moon-shimmered surface of the Colorado before he heard the gentle sounds of its waters slowing after the run of the rapids.

'*Bello*!' Rosa Canales exclaimed excitedly, and vented a shrill laugh of pure joy. 'Is it not a beautiful sight, Adam? Cool, clear water to drink. And even better, to bathe in.'

'You're not wrong,' Steele answered, and confined his expression of eager anticipation to a boyish grin – plus a rasping of the back of a hand across days old stubble that he hoped soon to be rid of.

Then the quarter of a mile wide river, their view of which had been restricted by the walls of the gorge, was briefly out of sight again: as the ground dropped down into a small hollow. And, as the two riders emerged on the opposite rim of the hollow, some hundred and fifty feet back from the bank of the river, the woman's burro snorted and stumbled.

Steele, who was riding slightly behind her to the right, shaped a curse with his lips. But had no time to utter it as he lunged forward and to the left. The move started when he spotted the unmistakable stab of light that was the muzzle flash of a fired rifle. The crack of the report coincided with the start of Rosa's shrill cry of alarm as she felt the shot burro begin to fall. And the cry changed to a short scream of pain as the Virginian crashed into her – one arm encircling her waist to both knock and wrench her out of the saddle. Steele, she and the burro hitting the ground at the same time. Just as a second shot cracked a bullet toward them. But this was less well aimed than the first and exploded chippings and dust from one of the gorge's rock walls as the man and the woman slid down the slope of the hollow. Away from one sprawled and inert burro up on the rim and toward the second animal, which had instinctively swung around to retreat from the violent disturbance.

Then, after a brief pause as the downslide was ended and Adam Steele became impassive while he continued to hold the trembling woman with one arm and to grip the Colt Hartford in the tight fist of the other hand, the rifleman directed six more shots into the gorge. Enraged, but not irrationally so as he unleashed the hail of bullets from his vantage point on the Arizona side of the Colorado – for he aimed the repeater fire at each rocky wall of the gorge, hopeful of hitting his targets with ricochets.

But when the volley was curtailed, the surviving burro vented a long and raucous snort that seemed to express depthless contempt for the shooter. While Rosa Canales rasped a string of what sounded like Mexican obscenities. And Adam Steele waited until she had run out of invective to growl:

'Seems a bloodbath is all that feller reckons we should have here, Rosa.'

'What can we do?' she gasped, as he made to withdraw his arm from her and she clutched his hand.

'Find a way to tell him no soap. But unless you let go of me, he'll maybe plug us before I can pull it on him.'

CHAPTER FIVE

IT WAS a time of high tension as the Virginian crawled up out of the hollow to begin back-tracking along the gorge. He was in deep moon shadow, but the sharpshooter on the far side of the river might well sense movement or simply suspect a withdrawal and elect to direct a second fusillade of rifle fire at the escape route just as Steele began to take it.

But there was no gunfire during the stretched seconds which formed into more than two minutes while he inched up and out of the hollow: not trusting the trickling and rippling of the slow moving Colorado to mask any sound he might inadvertently make in haste. Which would be unlikely to carry across the width of the river and up to the top of the low ridge where the rifleman was concealed. But there was a certain eeriness about this situation that had a disturbing effect on Steele once he was away from the Mexican woman who was almost petrified with fear at being left alone with just the surviving burro for company.

He was not terrified – in that direction experienced a degree of cold fear that served to heighten his readiness to retaliate against the danger. But he was unfamiliarly uneasy about an aspect of what was happening which he could not understand. And this disconcerting sensation remained with him after he had reached a point far enough back from the hollow where he should have felt it safe to move faster without any risk of being heard. But he continued to stalk rather than to hurry – eyes raking the dark night and rifle at readiness in a two-handed grip.

And it was not until he was back at the riverside again, the thunderous roar of countless tons of rushing water filling his ears and the foamy spume of the rapids stinging his face, that he was able to momentarily relax – and grin at his own foolishness.

All afternoon and into the evening he had been conscious of being followed by the lone rider he had first spotted in the desert heat shimmer before midday. And three times, while his companion on the trek toward the Colorado at first experienced a compulsion to talk and then became by turns happy with silence and joyful with song, he had visible proof of his suspicion of being followed. On occasions when the horseman on their trail made the mistake of allowing himself to be glimpsed.

Never nearer than a mile, though. So how had he managed to get ahead of Steele and Rosa Canales, cross the river and find a perfect spot from which to sharpshoot them? Perfect, anyway, had he been content to bide his time and make his attack when they were far out in the open. Unless it was a different man to the one who had been trailing them – which was a possibility he considered only briefly. And he was not prepared to reconsider as he grinned at himself as he stood beside – and far above – the white water of the torrenting Colorado. At the point where the north-eastern arm of the valley became a forked gorge reached the river – the ground having sloped upwards towards the roaring sound of the rapids instead of downwards to reach the Colorado where it flowed, shallow and serene, perhaps a mile and a half downstream to the south.

Here, the river was no wider than fifty feet. And a lot deeper than it was wide where it was forced to gush between the sheer walls of rock at a reckless speed and with a deafening din for several hundred feet. With, where the dry gorge intersected the lower and water-filled one, a natural arch bridge spanning the river between the California and the Arizona sides. Broad and deep at the tops of the facing cliffs, but just a few feet wide and looking to be wafer thin for perhaps ten feet at the centre of the span – seemingly ready to shatter under the lightest of weights so that whatever applied the breaking strain would be plunged twenty feet through spray-laced air and into the foamy white torrent beneath.

So the bridge was wide enough – and must have been strong enough – for the man and his horse to get safely across. After riding fast along the gorge with the upgrade, the thunder of the rapids masking the thud of galloping hooves. The man would have been on the Arizona side of the river before Steele and the woman even saw the moonlight glinting on the surface. Then needed to race his mount again, south to the point where the Colorado was forded at the trail. There to wait and watch with mounting impatience for his targets to come within the sights and range of his repeater.

Now it was the Virginian's turn to cross the river by the natural bridge. With never a look down and no change of pace, so that he never knew when he was on the most perilous stretch – which might have signalled an impulse to panic. But he could not evade the unbidden images of himself as the weakest section of the arch broke and he plunged downwards, arms flailing and legs kicking; to enter the deadly water and be dragged under, killed within seconds so that it would be a corpse that was spewed out at the lower end of the rapids – perhaps battered and bleeding from the impact with submerged rocks – to slow to the speed of the water's flow.

Then he sensed the time of this danger was over, and that the spume of the white water had ceased to lash at him. It was just sweat beads, much warmer, that coursed across his face and pasted his clothing to his body. But this dried quickly – the sweat of tension rather than exertion – as he turned southwards to move along a rocky strip between a band of mixed timber and the top of the cliff.

His thought processes were entirely rational now and he

was able to cast his mind back and work out a rough time schedule from the moment he had extricated himself from Rosa's hold and started out of the hollow.

Thirty minutes at the most, the larger part of it used up by his snail's pace progress away from the river. Now he moved much faster alongside the Colorado – high above it at first but always on a downgrade as he approached the lower end of the rapids. The river and thus also his path always gently curving – until he was in sight of the mouth of the gorge where Rosa Canales was hiding in the hollow.

Or maybe was dead if the sharpshooter's patience had run out again and he had risked crossing the river by the ford to check up on the reason for the silence. For the Virginian had told the woman to keep quiet and to stay down below the rim of the hollow until he came to get her. So what if she had heard somebody approach and rose to meet him and . . .

The Virginian's lips formed a curse that remained unspoken as he drove the impulse to futile conjecture out of his mind. And angled away from the bank of the river where the water began to slow toward serenity. He no longer did more than glance at the mouth of the gorge on the other side – and this just to check on his bearings when the wooded terrain allowed him the opportunity: needed to do this so that he could visualise this Arizona side as he had seen it from the hollow when the muzzle flash fleetingly alleviated the darkness. For it was essential he get behind and, if possible, above the spot where the sharpshooter was positioned.

And suddenly, it no longer mattered.

Steele was certain he was some way from achieving his initial objective when he glimpsed a movement far removed from where he estimated the shot that killed the burro had been fired – below and to the left of there. Below and to the right of where he froze between a tree and a rock, staring fixedly through the night as he swung the Colt Hartford to draw a bead from the hip on the man he could now see clearly

– as a darkly silhouetted figure against the moon-whitened trail.

Just a short length of the trail was visible from where the Virginian stood, raising the Colt Hartford to rest the stock to his left shoulder and his cheek to the stock as he thumbed back the hammer. Some fifty or sixty feet of it between the edge of the glinting water and the bulk of the timber clad rise on which the sharpshooter had earlier been concealed – and on which Adam Steele was now positioned, rifle aimed for a clear shot at the man over a range of no more than a hundred and fifty feet. A man who was short of stature and slight of build. Dressed in dark clothing that would have helped to hide him against the hillside but now acted to delineate him starkly on the trail, as he took short and slow steps toward the river: holding his repeater in a two-handed grip, aimed from the hip at the darkness beyond the mouth of the gorge on the other side. His progress extremely cautious, which was to be expected in the circumstances as he attempted to lure an unseen enemy out into the open. But there was something else about his gait that gave the Virginian pause for thought as his forefinger took first pressure against the trigger of the Colt Hartford. And drew a low grunt from him when he realised the man's slowness was not dictated solely by the need to take care. Pain was also a factor.

The man came to a halt a few feet back from the water's edge as Steele reached this conclusion about him. And perhaps two seconds later Rosa Canales yelled:

'Adam, he is coming! The *asesino* will get to me – '

'*Rosa, expliqueme por favor* – ' the man on the trail began before the woman was through.

And, as both curtailed their pleas, the Virginian called, loudly but even-toned: 'Drop the rifle, feller, and let's talk this over!'

'Adam, *gracias a Dios*!' Rosa Canales cried.

'*Hijo de puta*!' the man snarled, and vented a shrill moan of pain as he whirled away from the river. And began to trigger shots with the Winchester long before he had brought it to bear on a target.

The first bullet cut into the surface of the river, the second ricocheted off a boulder on the bank and a third thudded into the trunk of a tree part way up the hillside. Against the dry cracks of the shots, the sounds of the bullets impacting, the metallic clacks of the repeater's action being pumped and the despairing moans of pain and rage from the gaping mouth of the man below, Steele had time to yell:

'Hold it, you crazy – '

But then the lever action was pumped again and he knew he was in danger of taking the bullet that had been jacked into the breech of the rifle. And so he squeezed the trigger of the Colt Hartford. With time to take careful aim and so to place his shot – into the right shoulder of the man. With the object of disabling him and knocking the fight out of him. And for a stretched second it seemed this had happened. For the thudding impact of the .44 calibre bullet against and into his flesh halted the man's turn and stayed his finger on the trigger of his repeater. And he swayed backwards as his venting of pain and anger was interrupted – would doubtless have fallen had he not splayed his feet wide apart and kept himself erect by an effort of sheer willpower.

'Drop the rifle and – ' the Virginian started.

'*Vete al cuerno*!' the man snarled, and got off another shot.

It was a wild shot that by chance hit the rock beside Adam Steele: and erupted chips that sprayed in all directions. Several toward the Virginian, one of which hit his cheek. And stung without breaking the skin: causing him very little pain. But sensation enough to signal a vivid memory of what he had suffered after he got shot for the first time in his violent life.

He reacted instinctively now – in the context of one gunman facing another perhaps reacting in such a way for the first time since he fought in the war. He took cool and careful aim at his target – this time the hatless head of the man below. A man who was swaying again, and doing a macabre dance on slow dragging feet to stay upright – while his hands fumbled with the lever action of the rifle that waved wandlike in the air.

And he squeezed the trigger without an iota of compunction: totally uncaring about the motives of the man which earlier he had been so intent upon discovering, and merciless in his certain knowledge that if the man was able to raise his rifle he would not be able to hold it steady at the aim.

Then it was over.

The man killed instantly by the bullet that smashed through his skull at the crown of his head and lodged in the brain. He dropped his rifle with the lever action hinged loosely down from the frame, and sprawled out backwards with his arms flung to the sides and his legs still splayed. All this taking place while the memory of the Colt Hartford's report continued to ring in the ears of Adam Steele and the killer's grin remained fixed upon his heavily bristled, time and suffering lined face.

Then he blinked, pursed his lips and vented a low, terse whistle. Took his rifle down from the aim and thumbed open the loading gate as he held the hammer at half cock and turned the cylinder. Extracted both expended shellcases before he delved into a pocket of his oversize pants to bring out two fresh bullets – pushed them into the acrid-smelling chambers, returned the hammer and the loading gate and canted the Colt Hartford to his shoulder. Only then began to pick his way cautiously down the hillside to where his victim lay spreadeagled on the trail just short of the ford.

'Adam?' Rosa Canales called from out of the gorge on the other side of the river, and drew no response from the Virginian as he halted beside the corpse. And saw he was a Mexican of twenty-five or so, who had tried to appear older by growing a moustache. Good looking in a callow way, his lean features marred by acne. His black hair was slick with grease and now matted with blood. There was fresh blood, too, on his black leather vest in the area of his right shoulder. The blood on the lower portion of the vest and on the front of his cotton pants was congealed for the most part – but his recent movements had erupted some more crimson wetness when the old gut wound was opened up.

'Adam?' thc woman called again, in a tone that was demanding and a little angry.

'What is it?' he answered with a glance over the river, to where she could now be seen at the mouth of the gorge, leading the burro by the reins.

'I should come across now? It is safe for me to do so?'

'Reckon so,' he answered, taking less interest in the woman than in the animal and what it carried. Saw with a curt nod of satisfaction that she had unloaded the dead burro of packs and canteens which were now an additional burden to the surviving beast.

Then he raked his gaze over the high skylines to either side of the gorge, with scant hope of seeing any sign of the man who had been trailing them. A different man from this one, that was for sure. For he had been shot in the belly at least a day ago and could not possibly have travelled so far – and sometimes so fast – as would have been necessary to achieve what at first Steele had suspected him of doing.

Next the Virginian took his bearings again and, continuing to ignore the woman who was now up to her breasts in the river, started to climb the slope toward the point where the young Mexican sharpshooter had been hidden. And he was at the place, holding aloft a flaring match, when a cry of alarm from Rosa Canales distracted his attention. But she had merely tripped on a riverbed obstacle and for a few moments was completely submerged – until her head broke the surface and she was no longer afraid as she held on to the swimming burro, content to be towed across the deepest section of the ford.

So Steele returned to his investigation of the area behind some rocks and prickly brush where the latest victim of the Colt Hartford had spent so many hours. Smoking more than two dozen cheroots, not bleeding over much, ridding himself of the waste products of his body and maybe playing some kind of game with five perfectly round pebbles. If he had eaten while he waited, there was no sign of it. Probably he had gone down to the river occasionally to drink. There was nothing else to be seen here: and no point in entering into conjecture.

He was careful to see that the match was completely out before he dropped it and returned to the trail, reaching it just as Rosa Canales and the burro emerged from the river, soaking wet and shedding the excess water. The animal resigned in the manner of his kind to being subjected to this new discomfort. While the woman used both hands to wring out her hair, fist water from her eyes and bang each ear in turn.

'I think he called me a sonofabitch and then told me to go to hell,' Steele said flatly, trying to keep his gaze fixed on her face with the hair plastered across it – and not to look at the way the sodden shirt was pasted to the cones of her breasts with their extended nipples.

'That is right, Adam,' she allowed, her tone and her expression solemn. 'And I think you are now about to say that you do not need to have an understanding of low Spanish to hear that also he called me by my name?'

'Does his name matter, Rosa?'

She shrugged her shoulders and the gesture may well not have been designed to move her fabric-contoured breasts in such a sensual manner as it did. 'To him and those who loved him, I am sure, Adam. I feel sad that I do not know it . . . no, that is wrong, I think. It is sad that I do not remember it.'

She gave him an up-from-under look, which perhaps meant she had been looking down at herself to make sure she was displaying her body to the best effect. He met her coy

gaze for a part of a second and then started forward. Which action frightened her so that she gasped and took a backward step. But he went to the burro instead of the woman – to check over the burdens that the animal carried.

'It is obvious that my father has sent men out to look for me, Adam,' she said quickly. 'This one saw you with me after you free me from the savages and – '

'Not him, Rosa,' Steele cut in as he saw that she had brought from across the river all the gear he had salvaged from the mare shot by the Apache brave. 'There are two of them.'

She shrugged again and this time seemed oblivious to the effect of the gesture on the firm cones of her breasts. Then she spoke as quickly as before, as anxious to get said what she wanted to before she forgot. 'Did I not say men, Adam? Two at least. Perhaps many more. This one . . . ' She paused and frowned for stretched seconds, then grunted. 'Jose, his name is Jose, I am certain. When he sees I am with a man, he thinks the worst. He try to shoot you, Adam. Not thinking that perhaps I might be shot, too. He is young. My father, he has offered *muchas recompensa* – the big reward – for anybody who bring back his only daughter, I think. And this man – this Jose – who is little more than a *muchacho* . . . he acts without thinking of the risk.'

'Okay, Rosa,' Steele said and there was weariness in both his voice and his actions as he pushed his rifle through one of the bedrolls on the burro and started to unbutton his oversize shirt.

'Adam?'

'I said it was okay. It could be the way you say it is – '

'I am guessing badly.'

'And this young feller could have been gut shot by another of your father's men. Or one of the Apaches who grabbed you. Or a road agent. Or he could have accidentally shot himself. And his mount . . . hell, just as many alternatives could have happened to that.'

'Adam?' she said again with the same tone and look of anxious confusion.

'It's none of my business, Rosa,' he answered as he eased the shirt out from under the waistband of his pants and took it off, baring his torso with the livid tissue of the recent bullet wound standing out starkly against the darker surrounding flesh of his upper right chest. 'Usually when a man takes a woman home he doesn't expect more than to screw her.'

'Adam, I am . . . ' she started, shocked as he started in to unfasten his pants.

'You I'm taking home for a price of five thousand dollars, Rosa. And for that kind of money, I wouldn't expect this thing to be a bed of roses with you – '

'You want me now, Adam? To take me here and now while I am in this cond . . . '

'I don't want you anywhere except at home,' he cut in as he loosened his belt and then sat down on a trail-side rock to take off his boots. 'And I don't want you in that way, if you understand what I mean?'

She swallowed hard, perplexed and unsure if she should be relieved or if he had said something in a language that was not her own which she had misunderstood. 'But, Adam, you're taking off your clothes!'

'What I'm doing, sure enough,' he agreed as he kicked off his boots and then eased up off the rock briefly to push down his pants – removed them with his hose as part of the same peeling process. Then stood up, naked in the moonlight and chill of the night – and patently not aroused.

And then she relieved her anxiety and embarrassment with a burst of shrill laughter. 'Ah, you are going to bathe, Adam!'

From beside the rock he had picked up a straight razor and a cake of soap taken from the saddlebag salvaged from his gear after his horse was put out of her misery.

'You've got it,' he told her, and put his back to her as he moved into the coldness of the slow-moving Colorado. And did not turn to look at the woman until, having gone into the river up to waist level, he lowered himself into a stoop so that just his head broke the surface. 'See, Rosa, there's something about this business that smells bad. And I'm not sure how much of a stink I've been making.'

CHAPTER SIX

JUST AS Rosa Canales had not wanted to rest up at the place where the Apache braves had captured her, so she had no wish to make night camp on the Arizona side of the Colorado near to where the young Mexican named Jose had been killed. And she pleaded with the freshly shaved and bathed Virginian that it would make no difference to how she felt about the place even if he tossed the corpse into the river so that the currents carried it far downstream.

So it was that they moved more than a mile into the Territory of Arizona before the camp was made, the fire was lit, a meal was cooked and they bedded down for the night – the woman still in the clothing she insisted was not damp enough to cause her discomfort. This response to a query he put, one of the few brusque comments she made during the time between Steele taking his bath in the Colorado and the two of them preparing to sleep beside the dying fire off the trail at the edge of another desert. She seeming to be almost as badly affected by the incident at the river as by what had happened when this man first made his appearance.

In the few minutes it took for the Virginian to get to sleep, he was aware of the woman on the other side of the dully glowing embers as she tossed and writhed under her blankets. And while he listened to the sounds of her restlessness he was briefly resigned to undergoing a similar struggle for sleep should his mind dictate that it was to dwell on the way Jose had died. But it appeared he was allowed a clear conscience on that score, for he was suddenly oblivious – and awoke with a feeling of well being to the sight of filtered sunlight, the smell of coffee ready for drinking and the sound of Rosa Canales sneezing.

'Not inclined to say bless you to somebody I warned would catch a cold if she didn't take off the wet clothes – '

'Hey don't you talk to me like that, Adam,' the woman cut in, sounding in a good humour. 'You could be my father when you do. I think that him always giving me so much advice was one reason I left home. I have not madc breakfast. Just coffee.'

'Just coffee is fine,' he told her as he sat up and set his hat squarely on his head again.

She had poured a cup while she was speaking and now thrust it toward him, smiling brightly and apparently completely recovered from the ordeal at the Colorado River crossing. There was even a kind of underplayed exuberance in the way she moved as she returned to her side of the fire and sat down to finish her coffee: the smile of delight still firmly in place as she gazed this way and that – like she had just been unburdened of a great weight of concern that had blinded her to everything that existed outside of her private purgatory. And in the wake of this she derived enormous pleasure from the mere fact of being aware of her surroundings once again.

Then, suddenly, she was shamefaced as she saw that Adam Steele was watching her with a direct and appraising gaze. And she chewed on her lower lip for a few moments before she said defensively:

'I cannot help feeling good just to be alive. Perhaps it is wrong for me to feel so. Poor Jose, if only there had been the opportunity to talk to him . . . before the shooting and he was killed. If, as you say, Adam, there is another of my father's men following us, we should make plans to speak with him, do you not think so? It would be most tragic if there is more killing.' She shrugged her shoulders and again the gesture had a sexually attractive effect on her body. But on this occasion, Steele was certain, she was not conscious of it. And the smile which reappeared on her unlined face was free of any underlying meaning – exuded only happiness, pure and simple. 'But now I have no wish to think of bad things which could happen in the future, Adam. Just as I have no feeling to remember how it was with the savages and poor Jose. If that is wrong, I am sorry. But it is how I am. Perhaps because I am young, uh? Do you never wake up on such a day as this . . . and for no better reason than you are alive and the world is a beautiful place, feel that you could *brincar de gozo*? That you could jump for joy, Adam?'

She set down her cup and got to her feet, stretched her arms high into the air and stared skywards between them as she shuffled around in a full turn. And in such an attitude the entire length of her slender body was tantalisingly displayed at ever changing angles as the fabric of her shirt and pants was pulled taut over its firm, young curves.

For long moments, Steele eyed her and was aware of a dryness in his throat that could not be quenched by coffee. This as he saw the Mexican woman as she was and recalled how she had been twice before – first staked out spread-eagled on her back and then with the sodden clothing pasted to her flesh. Finally, as he needed to force himself to get to his feet after he emptied the grounds from his cup on the fire, saw briefly in his mind's eye an image of the interior of a Studebaker wagon and Julia French.

'Rosa,' he said and welcomed the time it took her to emerge from her reverie – time he used to get the thickness out of his tone.

'Something is wrong, Adam?' She looked and sounded a little afraid of him.

'Not with you,' he answered and had to make an effort to keep from sounding embittered as he began to break camp.

'You do not wish for me to show my feelings, Adam?' she asked, sullen now, after she had watched him for perhaps a half minute.

'Feelings are fine, Rosa.'

There was a longer silence between them now, during

which he distanced himself from her by becoming totally absorbed in the chores of loading the burro while she watched him with a puzzled frown taking a firmer grip on her face. Until she suddenly caught her breath, then vented a subdued moan.

'Something, Rosa?' he asked as he came upright after testing the tension of the cinch beneath the belly of the docile animal.

'You have the desire for . . . ' She blushed, swallowed hard and hung her head to avoid meeting his level gaze.

'You've got it,' the Virginian drawled as he picked up the reins of the burro and began to lead him out on to the trail to the east.

'Been a long time since I last had that kind of jump for joy. Which is no fault of yours and maybe none of mine, neither. Right now, though, you could make things a little easier for me by not posturing like a two dollar whore outside her crib every time I happen to look at you.'

'I do not do this!' she said quickly, defensively angry. 'If you think I am doing this, it is all in the mind of a man who – '

'You could be right, Rosa,' he interrupted, not loudly, but insistently. 'So maybe it'll be best if you and I finish this trip the way we are now?'

She was some ten paces in back of the burro being led by the Virginian. And had been closing the gap before he accused her of flaunting her body. But now she took pains to maintain the distance between them as she began to speak in fast, rasping Spanish. Her face contorted by anger until she became frustrated with directing such a high and draining emotion toward the unresponsive man leading the burro – who turned his head every now and then but obviously not to look at her. Instead, was again maintaining his routine but nonetheless conscientious surveillance over the heat-hazed desert terrain they were crossing.

'I was saying,' she went on after a lengthy pause, 'that

perhaps these few steps between us are not enough. And perhaps when we need to rest for the night again, it should be in two separate places?'

'That won't be necessary, Rosa,' Steele answered. 'And this gap is wide enough. I said it would be easier, is all, if you acted a little more strait-laced.'

'You did not say that, Adam!' she said sharply. 'You accused me of – '

'Okay, I'm sorry. It's what I meant. But I reckon I'm maybe asking for the impossible. You looking the way you do and me feeling so horny.'

She was silent for a few seconds, then spoke in contrite tone. 'I, too, make the apology to you, Adam. And will try to take the care to act with the *decoro*, the *correccion.* I think you say, the propriety, no?'

'You have it, Rosa.'

There was another pause, during which he looked in her direction once but not at her – peered back along the trail they had covered this morning and failed to see any sign of the man who was doubtless still following them. Then the woman suggested:

'Perhaps it will help if you think of me only in terms of the money I am worth to you when you return me to my home, safe and unharmed. My father, who will pay you the five thousand dollars I have promised, he has the saying about how he got to be so rich – he never mixed the business with the pleasure. Americans say the same, do they not, Adam?'

'Sure, Rosa,' the Virginian confirmed sardonically. 'That kind of money on your head makes you a higher priced piece of tail than I can afford.'

'*Hijo de puta*, I try to be understanding of how you feel and still you talk about me as if you think of me as the *ramera*!'

Steele glanced up at the brightly blue sky with its meagre scattering of small and high clouds. And ran the back of a forearm across his forehead to wipe off the sweat beads. Then looked back exclusively at the woman, to display a brief boyish grin as he told her: 'Truce, Rosa? It's not you giving me the hots anymore.'

She remained miffed at him for a few more moments. Then relented to the extent of making a face at him just before he returned his attention to the trail ahead. Then asked for an assurance.

'You say this now, Adam. When you must contend with the hardships of our journey. But when we have the day behind us and are in our camp for the night, will you be able to keep in your mind the saying of my father?'

'Make you a deal, Rosa?'

'A deal, Adam?'

'If you don't give me the business, I won't try to give you the pleasure.'

'*Comico*!' she said in a sarcastic tone and this heralded a long silence between them: during which the Virginian started out to call himself every kind of a fool for allowing himself to be infatuated by Rosa Canales who was a woman he knew he would not have glanced twice at in normal circumstances – and then he put her out of his mind as he faced up to problems more pressing than the desire to get laid.

While he was castigating himself for indulging in carnal thoughts about the woman, he continued to pay her more attention than the backdrop against which she moved whenever he scanned the seemingly empty-of-life terrain to the west. And saw that she continued to be both angry at him and wary of him. But after he had got his lustful desire for Rosa Canales into very small perspective in relation to the potential dangers which threatened the woman and himself, he no longer cared enough about her as anything more than five thousand dollars on the hoof to even with a passing glance try to guess at her mood.

There were no trees nor any clumps of brush high enough

to provide shade at noon, and so Steele pressed on – without complaint from the woman – to a low mesa where they stopped toward mid-afternoon to rest and to eat a meagre meal of hard tack and corned beef. The unappetising food was washed down with a little water. The burro fended for himself on some arid and dusty desert vegetation and snorted his dismay at the small amount of water the Virginian allowed him to drink.

But Rosa continued to be stoically uncomplaining about the discomfort and deprivation of the desert travel. Not quite sullen in her silence and tautly co-operative whenever Steele spoke to her – to call a halt, tell her to eat and drink, to suggest they move on again. And, after they had set off along the arrow-straight trail, when he asked of her over his shoulder:

'You said Phoenix was five days on the back of a burro from the river, Rosa.'

'*Si.*'

'But there are some smaller towns in between?'

'No, not towns. Places. A farm or a ranch, a stage line station.'

'Where we can get fresh water and restock our food?'

'*Supongo que si.*'

'What?'

'I suppose so.'

'You just suppose so?'

Now he looked back at her specifically and, as had happened at the stopping place in the shade of the mesa, he experienced no stab of desire at sight of the way that sweat pasted the damp-stained shirt to her breasts. Breasts that again moved tremulously when she wrapped her shoulders under the blanket which draped her head to keep the sun from burning her.

'We were well supplied from Phoenix, Adam. There was no need to stop at – '

'We?'

She sighed. 'The burros and I, Adam. A woman alone with her two animals. I was not unfamiliar with how some men are stirred by the sight of me . . . before the savages and then you made . . . And so, never knowing what kind of people were in these places along the trail, I did not stop at them to perhaps make trouble for myself. Phoenix, though, is a town where a woman may walk alone – '

'Sure, Rosa. Grateful to you.'

On the trail behind them there was just the sign left by the burros, the man and the woman. While ahead of them the often difficult to define way across the desert was unmarked except for the tracks in the dust of snakes, tiny animals and even smaller insects. The sign left by the woman and her two animals, Jose, the mystery rider who had not shown himself all this day and whoever else had used the trail – recently and way back to those who first trod it to make a trail – had been eradicated by time and weather.

The heat went out of the day and the rapid evening of the desert gave way to night. There was no place to shelter, so they had to make camp in the open. Which was not a hardship once the fire was roaring and the cooking smells filled the otherwise sagebrush-scented desert cold air.

If the mystery rider was within a few miles of where the Mexican woman and the Virginian bedded down – she distancing herself in spirit much further away than the other side of the fire from him – he did not have a fire to wisp smoke up into the moon and star bright sky.

The next morning, Steele was first to awake, and roused Rosa with a gentle prod with the rifle muzzle. And handed her a cup a quarter filled with the no longer good-tasting water from the Colorado River.

'We have coffee, I saw – ' she began.

'Coffee needs hot water,' he cut in on her. 'And hot water gives off steam that's just water going to waste. And we don't have enough of it out here to waste.'

'*Lo siento*. I am sorry, Adam.'

'Don't be. Just take everything as easily as you can. Emotionally and physically.'

'*Si.*'

'Be ready to leave as soon as the burro is loaded.'

'I must first . . . ' She let the sentence hang unfinished and looked down at her hands as she dry washed them.

'Sure, Rosa. But you have to make do without water.'

He was careful to always keep his back toward her as he broke the camp, and only looked up from the chores that engaged him to peer out across the near barren landscape – searching far and near for potential danger, or a possible friend in need, before the newly risen sun got high and hot enough to lay a circle of shimmering heat haze to close in the horizons. But there was no sign of life to be seen in any direction and it remained so for the entire morning and an hour into the afternoon. Which was when, after he had re-corked the canteen and gestured for the woman to get on her feet at the end of a perhaps fifteen minute rest break, he did a double take out along the eastern stretch of the seemingly endless trail.

'Adam?' Rosa Canales rasped, ready to be anxious or relieved as she questioned him about the first emphatic reaction he had made toward anything since they had started out on today's trudging journey.

'Here.'

Without it ever seeming to be stupid or even childish, they had never since he had spoken of his attraction to her got closer than arm's length to each other. Now, excited by his mood, she came up alongside him to follow with eager eyes the direction in which he pointed.

'Up ahead. Just before the haze blurs everything. Can you see a building?'

She stared hard, blinked several times, glanced at him to see that he was still gazing into the far distance and looked that way again. Then said: 'No, Adam. I see nothing. It is the *espejismo*, perhaps?'

The Virginian continued to concentrate on the point several miles to the east for perhaps another ten seconds, and remained tense for this time. Then he allowed: 'If that's Spanish for mirage, I reckon you're right, Rosa.'

'Mirage, *si.* But when we are closer, perhaps it will be that you were right at first.'

And they set off again, the woman with the blanket worn like a mantilla now walking level with the man in the over-size clothing – but with the burro he led between them. The animal as miserably docile as always while Rosa Canales and Adam Steele had to make a conscious effort to contain the urge to run forward. And perhaps defeated the object by losing as much sweat from high tension as they would have done had they moved any faster.

Then the woman blurted: 'I see it! Adam, it is as you said!'

She nodded several times and swallowed hard as the Virginian placated:

'Easy, Rosa.' But he allowed his feelings outlet in the form of a smile on his heavily bristled face.

'That is right,' she agreed. 'It is perhaps a place that was abandoned. And if nobody is there, there will be nothing we need. Except some shade, perhaps.'

There was a catch in her voice as she finished – as she talked herself into a fast letdown from elation and came close to bursting into tears. But then she saw that Steele's face – like her own beginning to be marked by the blistering and peeling ravages of sunburn – still wore the smile: and that it had perhaps brightened.

'Adam?' she said simply but implied much more as she swept her eager gaze between the man and the building.

'Could almost wish that black cloud was bringing rain, Rosa,' the Virginian replied. 'But I reckon it's smoke.'

She stared hard, rubbed her fists in her eyes like somebody newly awakened and looked again. Saw the smudge of nebulous darkness above the lighter coloured heat shimmer and gasped as she crossed herself: '*Gracias a Dios.*'

But she did not confine her expression of gratitude to this – offered up a lengthy, low voiced prayer in her own language with her eyes closed and one hand splayed over her breasts while with the other she gripped the bridle of the burro for guidance. And when she opened her eyes again it was to see that Adam Steele had slid his Colt Hartford from the centre of his bedroll and was carrying it canted to a shoulder, thumb resting on the hammer.

'*Que pasa*, Adam?' she rasped.

'I'm not saying you're wrong to give thanks to heaven, Rosa,' the Virginian replied evenly as he continued to peer fixedly ahead, familiar impassiveness having replaced the smile on his element-punished face. 'But I just reckon to be ready if this turns out to be one hell of a place.'

CHAPTER SEVEN

THREE RIDERS appeared suddenly on the trail. Then three more. And another three. Sitting without visible movement astride unmoving horses out front of the building on the north side of the trail – a building that came into gradual focus in the same way as the three ranks of men and mounts.

'*Militar*,' Rosa said, and vented a short laugh of relief as Steele, too, saw the uniforms of the cavalrymen to confirm what he had guessed from the disciplined way the nine men and mounts held ranks out front of the single storey adobe building.

A roofless building with narrow, arch-topped windows and what seemed to be the remains of a former tower at one end.

'Reckon you're a religious woman, Rosa,' the Virginian said as they closed to within a half mile of the cavalry troopers and the building with just an occasional wisp of smoke rising from inside the roofless walls.

'*Si*, Adam, *un poco*. A little. Not so much as I would – '

'Religious enough to know what a church looks like. Even a fallen down church.'

'Adam, I do not understand – '

'Just that I'd have thought,' he cut in on her nervous protest, 'that you'd have recalled the last place you passed before you reached the Colorado was a church. A fallen down one without even any holy water still in the – '

'I tell you that we avoid – '

'That's right, you did,' he interrupted her again, in the same weary tone. And sighed before he added: 'Guess it's of no consequence anyway.'

'Sir, ma'am!' one of the uniformed men called just as the woman was about to augment her angry argument against the Virginian's implication that she was lying to him. 'Afternoon to you. Captain Duff heading a patrol from Fort Curry.'

The Virginian waited until the gap had closed from a hundred feet to fifteen before he raised a hand to touch the brim of his hat and reply: 'Captain. This is *Senorita* Canales. I'm Adam Steele. Is the fort very far from here?'

The captain was a distinguished looking man of about fifty which made him about twice the age of most of the men in his patrol – a sergeant, two corporals and six troopers. All of them neat and clean and smartly turned out. Sitting well soaped and polished saddles on horses that had been recently and expertly curried. The entire troop bronzed by the Arizona sun, well fed and content with their lot. Most of them disdainful of the sorry state of the civilians and none of them considering that Rosa, looking as she did now, was worth more than a glance in terms of her being a woman.

'Ten miles to the south-east, Mr Steele. The ladies are never expert at directions and distances, are they?'

The woman rasped a Spanish curse that was not loud enough to carry to the mounted men. And then had to force a fit of coughing to keep herself from venting more of them and louder. Then she fumbled a canteen off the saddle of the burro and uncorked it – had to tilt it vertically and tip her head to drain the final drops of water from it.

'The *senorita* has had a touch of the sun, Captain,' Steele explained. 'Been a rough trip from the Colorado on foot. After I had to put down the other burro when he went lame.'

'Whatever you say, Mr Steele,' Duff allowed after briefly revealing his suspicion of the circumstances and then deciding that they were of no concern to the army and therefore of no interest to him. 'A half mile east of the old church here, a dry wash crosses the trail. If you follow that, it'll bring you to Fort Curry. We can spare you some water. Food appears to be unnecessary. If you had arrived earlier, it would have been my pleasure to share a hot meal with you. Santori, pass your canteens to the civilians. You will have a share of everyone else's water for what remains of this patrol.'

'Sir!' the lean and mean-faced sergeant rapped out, moving his horse out from between the officer and one of the corporals, unhooking his two canteens from the saddle as he did so.

'Grateful to you,' Steele said as he accepted the water from the non-com who, with his back to the captain, scowled his dislike at having to surrender the near full canteens.

'My pleasure,' Santori lied. 'Just leave them at the post, uh?'

'Be happy to.'

The sergeant backed his mount skilfully into its former position and the captain threw up a textbook salute. Said:

'*Senorita* Canales, Mr Steele. Happy to have been of service to you. Necessary now for the patrol to continue. Since you have adequate water to see you through, there is nothing to cause you concern between here and the fort.'

With the hand that had executed the salute, Captain Duff now signalled an order for the men to move forward with their mounts held to a walk. And they held ranks on the move almost as precisely as when they were halted out front of the ruined and abandoned church in which the final ember of the cooking fire had now gone out.

Steele, with the rifle still canted to his shoulder but no longer with a thumb on the hammer, moved to the right and took the burro after him. Rosa came too, since she was still gripping bridle. Thus, the troopers did not have to veer off the trail to by-pass the two civilians and their animal. Although a number of them, disdainfully proud of their neatness and cleanliness that was emphasised by the appearance of the civilians, looked as if they wished Duff had led them on a wider swing around Steele, the woman and the burro.

'All the men at that post as high and mighty as that bunch?' the Virginian asked in a sour tone as the puffs of dust raised by the easy walking cavalry mounts settled back on the trail in the wake of the patrol.'

'I can explain, Adam,' she said huskily.

'Two questions are all I need answers to right now,' he told her, tugging on the reins of the burro and heading with the animal toward the crumbling arch entrance of the church.

She held back and called to him when he stopped to look inside: 'His name was not Jose. It was Esteban. Esteban Chevez, the *vaquero* who worked for my father on De Raza Hacienda and who I tell you I fall in love with – '

'Question one,' Steele cut in as he cast a final glance in through the entrance of the church and then raked his equally unimpressed gaze over the outside. 'You really are the daughter of the rich owner of the Mexican ranch?'

Just neglect, the passing of time and the elements had destroyed the church – collapsing the tower, caving in the roof and crumbling and staining the walls. While countless cavalry patrols and civilian travellers following the trail had for many years used the shell of the building for rest and shelter. The appetising aromas of hot food and coffee mixed in with the taint of cooling fire ash still clung to the abandoned place as the soldiers moved away from it to the west and Steele – Rosa Canales quickening her pace to catch up with him – went in the opposite direction.

'*Si*, Adam!' she called shrilly, imploring him not to doubt this. 'I swear to it on my own life and that of my father whom I love dearly that I am who I said.'

'Question two,' he said coldly as the breathless, dripping with sweat woman resumed her former position on the other side of the burro.

'I will tell you everything, Adam.'

'Your Pa love you five thousand dollars' worth?'

'I tell you, he would pay much, much more for – '

'He had a bullet in the belly, Rosa. By my reckoning, five cents is too much. But then I'm not anybody's father.'

She began to weep, the tears spilling from the inside

corners of her eyes and coursing down her sunburn-scarred cheeks, picking up beads of sweat on the way. To reach her jawline and drip off to further darken the stains on the shirt adhering to the slopes of her breasts.

He ignored her and after several minutes she was through with the crying. But it was not until several more minutes had passed, and Steele had swung to the left to follow the south-eastern route of thc arroyo that she felt the desperate need to speak.

'Adam?'

'Yes, Rosa?'

'I know we have the ten miles still to go. But there will be much water there. We may have some of that which was given to you?'

'Sure,' he said as he came to a halt and the obedient burro matched his act.

'*Gracias*,' the dejected woman said, and it was apparent that she needed to work at not grabbing for the canteens, uncorking one of them and gulping down some water. But she was able to maintain a high degree of self-control and drank only a little of Sergeant Santori's good tasting water.

'You can have more, Rosa.'

'*Esta seguro del todo*?' she said, her dark eyes large with excitement.

'How's that again?'

'*Dispense usted.* I am sorry, Adam. I say, are you quite sure?'

'Sure I'm sure.'

She took another, longer drink. But was not greedy – obviously did not have as much water as she wanted before she re-corked the canteen and they started off again, following the course of the dry wash that was defined by not having any desert vegetation growing along the centre of its bed. And they were perhaps a third of the way to their destination of Fort Curry which was still hidden beyond the heat shimmer, when the woman once again found the silence between them too discomfiting and pleaded:

'I really wish to tell you all, Adam.'

'When we're out of the sun and are cleaned up, rested, fed and properly watered maybe,' the Virginian offered, halting the burro to take a drink himself and give one to the animal. But an invitation to the sullen woman was refused with a violent shake of the head under the mantilla-like blanket.

Then they moved off again and, as had been happening since they had left the crumbling church, Rosa Canales was disconcertingly aware that in maintaining his survey of their vast and empty environment, he allowed his eyes to linger on her with a brief change of expression in the depths of their darkness that made her skin crawl and caused her to feel hotter than any sun was capable of doing.

'You are sure you want nothing from me?' she demanded, on the brink of anger, when she felt she would explode with high tension if she did not have an outlet.

'I'm sure, Rosa.'

'Then I have just the one question for you, *gringo*!' She rasped out the final word to stress that she used it in its most derogatory sense.

'I have nothing to hide, Rosa.'

'I wish for you to tell me – when you keep looking at me, what you think you are looking at, *gringo*?'

Adam Steele ballooned his cheeks and blew out a stream of expelled breath. Answered with a slight shrug. 'You don't know either, uh?'

CHAPTER EIGHT

AS HAD happened in many instances of military establishments along the ever moving frontier, Fort Curry was an isolated outpost only in terms of being many miles from a neighbouring community in any direction. Years before, when the stockade fence had been erected and the various buildings were put up behind its protection, it had stood alone as the only man-made scar on the barren tract of terrain where the southern fringe of the scrub desert touched the northernmost rise of the Eagle Tail Mountains.

On the night when the Virginian, the Mexican woman and the burro reached it, Fort Curry was more of a small town with a military post as a part of it rather than a fort to which entrepreneur civilians had been attracted to supply the needs and wants of the soldiers detailed to serve at the post. Though that was how the small town had got started, Adam Steele was able to see as he was trailed by the burro and Rosa Canales under a pole supported sign that proclaimed:

FORT CURRY
TERRITORY OF ARIZONA
Boom town of the Eagle
Tail Mountains

The black-scorched lettering was faded by the suns of many years and the board which carried the legend was warped. Which was symptomatic of the boom which had never actually happened or had been short lived before it burst.

The army post was built on a levelled area some one

hundred and fifty feet up the slope of the first rise to the south of the desert's edge and the trail which became a street a few yards beyond the boastful sign rose steadily for about a half mile to the closed double gates in the spike-topped front stockade walls. Some fifty yards from the gateway – the gap probably left unfilled at the insistence of the United States Army – were the first of the earliest civilian establishments. These were adobe shacks which had maybe served many and varied purposes before they became the barber shop and the bank that they were now. Then, on either side of the street, was a row of stone, brick or timber built premises which had obviously been erected when times began to be good for Fort Curry. There was a saloon and a gunsmith's, a newspaper office and livery, a boarding house and a half dozen stores. And, as a pointer to what had promised the town might be something else than a civilian settlement outside an army post, an assay office. Which was boarded up and derelict now: as were the newspaper office, the gunsmith and four of the stores. Just those selling hardware and groceries remained in business. Closed at this time of night, though. On the lower slope of the street there were a few more adobe shacks, some of tin and even two canvas tents which had a look of permanence to them.

It was close to midnight when the newcomers started up the sloping street between the scattered homes of the gold grubbers who had never found the mother lode – past and present, for some of the places were quite obviously abandoned while others showed a gleam of light or had chimneys that wisped smoke. This smoke was all that moved in the night across this area after the man and the woman and the burro had passed through it – all that was visible, anyway. For the Virginian was able to sense watching eyes in turning heads tracking him along the centre of the broad street. Just as he was conscious of being under surveillance from higher up the slope – and not only by the two sentries on the walkway above the gates of the fort.

He could appreciate why these people were showing such an interest in him – citizens of a grimly forlorn community who would see few strangers outside of soldiers newly detailed to relieve men from the fort ordered elsewhere. And so he was less concerned by local interest in his progress than by the increasingly irritating certainty that he and Rosa Canales were still being followed by the mysterious lone rider he had first glimpsed at another place where a desert flatland reached a range of hills. First glimpsed, and then hardly ever seen again. Yet definitely somewhere out there on the back trail, skilfully remaining just beyond the heat haze during the day and just below the horizon at night.

Only once, as he and the woman and the burro had followed the dry wash from the main trail to the spur that angled out of the north-east to dead end at Fort Curry, had the sullenly angry Rosa Canales broken her morose silence, when she had taunted him: 'This man, if he follows us still, he is like the ghost, *gringo.* You are afraid of the *espectro*, uh? The way you are constantly looking over your shoulder is why I think this.'

'Don't reckon he could scare me to death,' the Virginian had replied. 'Just need to be sure he doesn't get close enough to try it some other way.'

Now, as they veered away from the centre of the street to head for the two-storey brick built boarding house between the false fronted Post House Saloon and the boarded up office of the *Eagle Tail Herald,* there was no trace of a mocking tone in the woman's voice as she shuddered and rasped: 'It is like the last time. This place, *me da grima hormigueo.* How you say . . . it gives me the . . . ?'

'Creeps,' he supplied.

'*Si.* Even in the full daylight with the sun shining. It is the way people – the men – look at me. I can feel their eyes upon me now, though I cannot see them.'

'Reckon women are spread thin on the ground hereabouts,' Steele explained with disinterest as he banged a fist on the door of the boarding house which was in total darkness. 'You and your *amigo* stay here when you were in Fort Curry before?'

He put his back to the door and looked around him as he spoke – saw the light in the saloon go out as a window on the upper floor of the boarding house was illuminated. And a woman could be heard, her tone complaining but her words not sounding clearly enough to be understood.

'We did not remain in this town,' Rosa Canales answered. 'Mexicans are not welcome here. The people are bigots. We buy the food we need and we leave. Not by the same way you and I come here. Further to the south, it must have been. For I had no knowledge of the ruined church where the soldiers were.'

Her tone had changed to something close to ingratiating as she attempted to lay some groundwork for an explanation of her motives.

'I said we'd talk later, Rosa,' Steele reminded her, returning his attention to the door as a chain rattled and bolts were slid – convinced the main interest being shown in him emanated from the saloon while the sentries above the fort entrance merely viewed the late night arrivals to town as amounting to no more than an insignificant break in the dull routine of their duty. And all the others in Fort Curry who had kept surreptitious watch on the strangers were for now content with what they had seen.

Until the fat woman wearing a nightdress and cap and carrying a candle in a holder swung open the door and greeted sourly: 'Not more foreigners?' Extended the light further across the threshold and moved it from side to side before she added: 'You was through this way awhile ago, girl. And you ain't from across the border, mister.'

'Need two rooms, ma'am,' Steele told her evenly. 'Two meals. Two coffees. Two tubs of hot water. Can you do that for us? If *Senorita* Canales promises to do what she can to act like an American?'

The Mexican woman shot a suspicious glance at the Virginian and saw that his sarcasm was directed solely at the boarding house keeper, who vented a harsh laugh before she replied:

'I tell you, mister, the way business is gettin' to be in this stinkin' town, I'll be happy to make that three of everythin' and you can bring in the donkey. Providin' you got the dollars to pay.' She shifted the candle again, so that its flickering light fell more on Rosa Canales than Adam Steele or the burro. And added with a sniff of disdain: 'Well, I reckon it's a lie to say I'd be happy.'

'Punetero aciana –'

'The livery stable still in business?' Steele asked to cut across the Mexican woman's embittered voice.

'Just, mister. Like this place.'

'So two of everything. Be back in a few minutes.'

'You'll have to attend to your animal's needs, mister,' the fat woman warned as Steele took up the reins of the burro and made to lead him away. 'On account of Mel Ivers runs the saloon and the livery both. And by this time of the night he's almost always swallowed so much of his own stock in trade he can't tell one end of a horse from the other. Come on inside, girl.'

'Hurry back, Adam,' Rosa called nervously as she stepped across the threshold.

And despite his current opinion of the woman, the Virginian experienced a mild stab of arousal triggered by her plea in which it was possible to hear – doubtlessly mistaken – a veiled invitation. But the moment was quickly gone, as lust was displaced by the far more familiar sense of animosity directed toward him from a different direction as the door of the boarding house thudded closed.

There was a disconcerting itch between his shoulder blades as he angled across the street to the livery, his back toward the undraped windows and still open doorway of the darkened saloon. While he strained his hearing to the almost painful limit and picked up no sounds beyond those made by the burro and himself.

With one of the double doors half open, enough blue moonlight shafted into the livery so that he was able to enstall the animal and ensure he had feed and water without need of a lamp to show him what he was doing. In the moonlight, also, he saw there were just two other stalls occupied: by well tended saddle horses which had been in the shelter and peace of the stable for long enough for any effects of their last outing to have faded. And he was able to see, too, that hung on a peg at the front of each of these occupied stalls was an ornate saddle studded with the kind of metallic decoration that suggested it was the property of a Mexican.

Steele hooked most of the burdens which had been carried by the burro on the appropriate peg and left the stable with just his rifle, the saddlebags and the canteens that Sergeant Santori had been ordered to loan him – both of these now empty.

When he closed the door, he was again conscious of enmity being tacitly directed toward him from the darkness beyond the open threshold of the saloon. And the same irritating itch between the shoulder blades made itself felt for several stretched seconds as he went up the street – an awareness and a sensation that remained strong enough to squeeze beads of the sweat of tension from his pores and caused him to maintain a more tight than usual grip on the rifle canted to his shoulder until he started across the fifty feet wide gap that divided the civilian community from the army post. When both sentries shifted their carbines to the aim and froze. But the Virginian with the sun-ravaged, heavily bristled and sweat-beaded face did not himself become immobile until one of the uniformed men snarled:

'Hold it, mister.'

There was perhaps one second of tense silence before the other cavalryman demanded: 'State your business at Fort Curry!'

Steele had the saddlebags draped over the crook of the elbow of his right arm and was holding the straps of the army issue canteens in his right hand. Now he raised that hand and moved it slightly so that the canteens swung from side to side.

'Met Captain Duff's patrol at the old church up on the main trail, feller. Was a little short on water. The captain had Sergeant Santori loan us his near filled canteens. The sergeant asked me to rcturn the canteens to the fort.'

The Virginian had suppressed the impulse to shout back at the highly placed sentries at the same level they had barked their orders: and as he made his even voiced response he felt the tension drain out of him. At the same time was sardonically aware of the discomfiture of the two soldiers who had over-reacted to his approach.

'So why the hell didn't you – ' the first of them to snap an order snarled.

'He just did tell us, Trooper!' the higher ranked cavalryman growled. And then, to Steele commanded: 'Cross to the gate and throw the canteens up here, mister.'

The Virginian complied with this, the canteens were caught at the first toss and he paused with his head tilted back to ask: 'You fellers are a little edgy, aren't you?'

'On your way, mister!' the junior man snarled softly.

'Our job is to keep the Apaches from running wild,' the other Fort Curry cavalryman augmented. 'Trouble between civilians that has nothing to do with the Apaches is not the concern of the military. Do like the trooper told you.'

'Thanks for nothing.'

'They're in Melvin Ivers' saloon. Two of them.' Not loud enough to carry beyond Steele.

'Like I said, feller, thanks for nothing,' Steele drawled to the higher ranking man as he turned and started back across the open length of street between the fort and the civilian community.

'So up your ass, mister!' the trooper snarled.

'Tell you something, Rosen?'

'Yeah, Sergeant?'

'Why I'm a sergeant and maybe will go higher and you're the lowest of the frigging low and won't ever get off the frigging bottom?'

'Sergeant?'

'Because you're frigging stupid is why. That civilian didn't mean thanks for nothing when he said it. I told him something he either didn't know or couldn't be sure of and he only said thanks for noth . . . '

Steele crossed the midway point between the gate of the fort and the earliest adobe buildings that had started to change a stretch of trail into a length of street. And in so doing moved out of earshot of the rasping whisper of the non-com's voice as the trooper was bawled out. For a few stretched seconds felt strangely detached from his surroundings. Then sensed watching eyes again. From the saloon, from the walkway above the gateway of the fort and from elsewhere along the short single street of the town that had failed.

A little animosity and a great deal of curiosity was how he judged the mix of interest as he came in off the open area and stepped at the same easy pace as before between the façades of the facing buildings: angling slightly to one side toward the boarding house where now the only lighted window was on the lower floor. A few more unhurried paces and the Virginian in the over-sized clothing, with the Colt Hartford canted to his left shoulder and his right arm burdened by the saddlebags off the burro, knew he could be certain that the cavalry sergeant was not mistaken in confirming what he had been reasonably certain of himself. And thus was Adam Steele able to discount the mass of attention directed toward him – to concentrate his wariness entirely upon the darkened but not closed-up Post House Saloon as he moved across the wagon-wide alley mouth between the abandoned office of the defunct newspaper and the undeserted and dangerous drinking establishment.

Silence was clamped in what seemed like a palpable grip over the entire community and had its purity marred only by the measured tread of one man's progress down the slope of the street. Until Steele was level with the open doorway of the saloon which, like the façade of the next door boarding house, was unstooped and had no sidewalk out front of it. When a man said softly from beyond the threshold:

'*Buenas tardes, primo.*'

'*Adios, Americano!*' the second Mexican snarled, louder and from further away.

Steele had snapped around just his head as the man inside the doorway completed the sardonic greeting. And was just starting to turn away from the waist as the man up on the roof was done with words: and began his attack.

The moon-shadowed interior of the saloon was pitch black to the eyes of the Virginian who, having shifted his surprised gaze away from the threshold to seek the second man, was unable to get a new bearing on the one inside the place now that he was silent again. And was able to keep the darkness of the doorway only on the periphery of his vision as he peered upward – at the man who suddenly rose from a crouch on the front edge of the saloon's roof. Was a silhouetted shape against the moon and star lit sky as he leaned slightly forward and flung his right arm downward. Something glinted at the end of the moving arm. And then was detached from it.

A knife that was sent spinning on its way by a powerful whiplash action of the throwing arm. Whatever sound it made as it sped through the night air masked by the grunt of satisfaction vented by the man who threw the knife.

At precisely the same instant the Mexican released the knife, the Virginian completed his turn to face the saloon doorway – and at the same time pushed both his arms into the air. The thud of his trailing foot to the surface of the street spaced an immeasurably short time from the less violent sound of the knife striking and sinking into one of the swinging saddlebags that protected his head. This sound in perfect unison with the click of the Colt Hartford's hammer as it was clicked back.

The grunt of satisfaction from the man up on the roof started to change tone to an animalistic snarl of frustration as he saw he had failed to hit his target. But there was just a part of a second for him to give vent to his abrupt change of mood before the crack of the rifle briefly swamped all other sound. The shot exploding a bullet into the underside of the snarling man's jaw, to force his mouth closed as it holed his tongue, tunnelled up through his palate, burrowed into and out of his brain and became trapped when its lessening velocity failed to allow it exit from his skull.

The man who had taken the bullet in his head was dead on his feet but had not started to collapse when the Virginian commenced his next move. Snapped both arms down and let go of the saddlebags as he squeezed the trigger of the already cocked rifle a second time. To fire a shot for effect into the darkened interior of the saloon a split second before he lunged for the wall to one side of the doorway. Heard a terse comment from the inky darkness that might have been a string of Spanish oaths or an expression of fear. The tone difficult to comprehend because the words were muffled: by the falling form of the dead man from the roof.

Then the man inside the saloon shrieked: 'Miguel!'

The calling of the name coinciding with the sickening crunch of Miguel's unfeeling body against the street. Head first. At this same time, too, another spinning knife sank into a wrong target – and could be seen buried to the hilt in the belly of Miguel as the corpse became sprawled on its back just outside the doorway of the Post House Saloon. On one side of the dead man the abandoned saddlebags with a knife in one of them dropped by Steele. On the other side, Steele himself – standing with his back pressed to the wall of the saloon, cocked rifle held in a two-handed grip angled across in front of him and head turned. Cracked eyes peering intently across the open doorway, but relying on his ears to provide the first warning that the second Mexican was nearing the threshold.

For what seemed a very long time, but could not have been more than a few seconds, the silence within the saloon was as complete as that clamped down over the town outside. But then there was a short burst of muffled sounds – like a man trying to speak against a gag. The Mexican snarled:

'*Callarse*!'

And the Virginian's sun-punished and thickly bristled face showed a fleeting frown of anger as a chorus of demanding voices was raised at the fort. For this din of harshly spoken questions and competing answers about the reason for the gunshot masked further sounds from inside the saloon. Until running footfalls hit hard on the floor of the place, the man heading fast for the doorway. When, impassive faced again, Adam Steele remained with his back pressed to the wall as he tightened the grip of his left fist around the barrel of the Colt Hartford and maintained first pressure on the trigger with his right forefinger.

There was still a great deal of noise at the fort as men in authority defeated their object by competing against each other in demanding at the tops of their voices for the two sentries up on the walkway to report.

Then the running man lunged out of the doorway and, at the instant he showed himself in the moonlight, the shouting at the army post was matched in volume by the civilian population of Fort Curry.

And the Virginian who an instant before had been ice cold at the peak of nervous tension was suddenly drenched in sweat – seemingly from the physical effort it required to stay his finger on the trigger of the Colt Hartford.

The running man was beyond the muzzle of the levelled, greasy feeling rifle then. And starting to fall forward – tripped by the bullet shattered and blood run face of Miguel. Unable to utter even a muffled sound of terror now: because that terror made him mute behind the leather belt that forced his mouth wide open and bit into his bulbous cheeks. And unable to break his heavy fall on top of the corpse because his wrists were bound together behind him.

Steele was unaware for a stretched second of anything that happened outside the periphery of what suddenly seemed to be his tunnel vision. This moment coming immediately after he saw the man was gagged and experienced something akin to intense physical pain at the effort needed to keep from shooting him.

Then a gun showed clearly at the very centre of his blinkered field of focus. A silver plated Tranter .45 revolver with a great deal of ornate engraving on the barrel and frame and cylinder. Reminiscent of the decoration on the saddles across in the livery. The butt of the Tranter in the grip of a black gloved hand at the end of a black sleeved arm. And Steele briefly recalled an image of Miguel as he took his head first dive off the roof – dressed all in black except where the solid colour was relieved by silvered buttons and stitching, hat band and belt buckle.

The gun was pressed straight out across the threshold at the centre of the doorway. Then began to track to the side where the Virginian stood – seemingly rooted to the spot, glued to the wall and too taut to move even the muscles of his right forefinger. And, for the briefest sliver of time, this was how it was for Steele as he recovered from the shock of almost gunning down an innocent and helpless man. Then, in the next instant decided that a quick death from a fatally placed bullet was too good an end for the man who had come so close to causing him this brand of torment once more.

And so, as the black clad and silver spangled Mexican loomed large on the threshold of the Post House Saloon, the sweat drenched Virginian shot him. At point blank range. Through the back of his gloved right hand. The bullet impacting with the butt of the Tranter after it had passed through his flesh, the force of this sending the gun arcing out of the suddenly loosened fingers to bounce on the street two yards away.

By which time the injured man had become as unmoving as Steele was a moment before. But with fear instead of fury in his pockmarked face as he held his injured hand with his good one at the base of his belly – the wound either numb or its pain suppressed beneath the weight of the primary emotion.

In the utter silence that now descended upon the grim little town where the desert met the hills, the dripping of blood from the bullet wound made audible splashing sounds on the boot of the Mexican – who suddenly gasped, like he had been winded by the gentle pressure of the muzzle of the Colt Hartford as Steele rested it on the ornate buckle of his gunbelt with its single, now empty, holster.

The bound and gagged man now began to make muffled sounds again around the belt across his mouth, the twenty strong line of mostly half dressed soldiers on the walkway at the fort started to talk – and to disperse back to their barracks. And there were some brief exchanges in the darkened town, before more of its citizens returned to what had occupied them before this rare break with mundane routine attracted their detached attention.

'*Senorita* Rosa Canales, I reckon, is the reason – ' Steele started evenly as he remained flat to the wall, with the cocked Colt Hartford aimed across his belly and at that of the fear-filled middle aged Mexican with the pitted face.

'*Senor, no hablo ingles*!' the Mexican blurted. '*Haga el favor de darme la hora* – '

'He says he does not understand you, Adam,' Rosa Canales said evenly as she emerged from the boarding house next to the saloon.

The fat woman who ran the place came behind her, a broad grin on her fleshy face as she waddled by the younger and more slender Mexican. And said with mock concern: 'There there, Mr Melvin Ivers. It's all over now. Your good friend Flora Waldorf will set you free.' Then she hardened her tone as she dropped into an unladylike squat beside the saloonkeeper to say: 'And maybe next time I'm short on cash and long on need, you'll give me friggin' credit, uh?'

Against the angrily muffled attempted retort of Ivers, Rosa Canales spoke an even more angry sounding burst of Spanish to the man with the gunshot hand. The man flinched several times, like the words she flung at him actually hit him. Then broke in on her, his dark eyes constantly switching from the woman to Steele and back again.

'*Hablo me no –* ' the Virginian growled with more than a hint of impatience at the fast talking Mexican.

'Your Spanish grammar is terrible, Adam,' Rosa accused, her tone almost light hearted and a half smile on her face.

'Like my English can be,' Steele rasped.

'I am sorry, Adam,' she said, grim faced and voiced again, both apologising for being amused and telling him she did not understand his cryptic comment.

'Tell him that what happened to him was just for starters.'

She looked hard at Steele, then shrugged and translated to the bewildered man who had recovered sufficiently from the depth of his terror to experience pain from his wound. But abruptly felt only fear again.

Melvin Ivers said croakily as he got to his feet: 'I wanna thank you, mister, for – '

'Tell him,' Steele cut in on the freed and trembling saloonkeeper, 'that I need to know the whole story of why he and his partner tried to kill me.'

Rosa translated again and after he had swallowed hard, the Mexican nodded several times. And opened his mouth to speak, but snapped it closed again when Steele said, his tone less harsh and the merest trace of a boyish smile on his face:

'And tell him not to be fooled by how nice and friendly I was to him when he first came out of the saloon.'

'*Simpatico*, Adam?' she said, and then her frown became a smile that was even more fragile than the one he wore as she added: 'You make another *broma pesada*, I think. One more of your sick jokes, I think?'

'Don't want the feller to get the wrong idea about me, Rosa,' the Virginian answered. 'Just because the first time we met I happened to holed his hand.'

CHAPTER NINE

THE MEXICAN'S name was Gregario Garrido and his dead partner had been Miguel Lozano. This much Adam Steele was able to elicit for himself from the opening burst of fast spoken Spanish. But then he picked out just the occasional word and had to trust Rosa Canales was giving him an honest account of what the older of the two knife men told her in response to the translated questions she asked of him.

The interrogation took place in the cramped dining room of Flora Waldorf's boarding house. While Steele and Rosa ate a late supper of cold cuts and sweet potatoes and the fat woman bathed then dressed the bullet-shattered hand of Garrido.

The wounded man who was too despondent about his own situation to grieve over the death of his partner and the tight lipped woman who tended his injury sat on a sofa in one corner of the cramped room. The Virginian and the Mexican woman were both seated on one side of the table. A fifth occupant of the room was the tall and flabby, late fifties in age Melvin Ivers. Who had been insulted that Steele turned down his invitation to talk, and drink, in the saloon, resented that it was left to him to go rouse the gold grubber who acted as town undertaker and who had gotten drunk in the Post House, to come take care of the corpse, sulked for awhile when Flora Waldorf started to tend the Mexican's wound instead of seeing to his own bruises, then got angry and began to suck from the bottle he had brought with him after nobody wanted to listen to what had happened to him when Adam Steele and Rosa Canales were seen entering Fort Curry. Ivers sat at the end of the long and narrow table.

'This man is Gregario Garrido and the one who you killed was Miguel Lozano,' Rosa explained after an exchange of Spanish in the wake of the Virginian's opening question. 'They have worked for my father in past years. When it has been necessary for him to hire on extra men at the time of the *rodeo* . . . this means something else in your language, I think. The . . . ?'

'Round up?' Steele suggested.

'*Si.* At the times of the round ups and the driving of the cattle to the market. This man I cannot recall, but I think I remember the other one.'

'More your age and better looking, I reckon. Ask him if he knows how many other knife throwing *vaqueros* your Pa hired on to round up this extra special maverick?'

'You liken me to a cow, *gringo*?'

Steele swallowed a mouthful of food, sighed and answered: 'Did I say cow, Rosa? Just ask him, uh?'

The woman's query was short, but the answer was long: Garrido looking anxiously at Rosa Canales several times while his wound was dried and dressed – as if he felt that much he was saying reflected badly upon her. But whenever he seemed on the point of faltering she nodded for him to continue. Merely compressed her lips and caught her breath on occasion. And finally lost her appetite before she was through with the supper and while the nervous Mexican was still talking. Then Garrido shrugged his shoulders a number of times and Rosa sucked in several deep breaths before she began to translate – a look of concentration on her burned and blistered and peeling face as she worked at recalling all the man had said.

'It seems I was wrong in putting a figure on how much Don Benito Canales values his only child, *gringo.* Not many times what I offer you to take me home. But precisely five thousand dollars. In dollars American, though. Not in the *pesos*, which is something, perhaps? *Como quiera que* – any how, Garrido and Lozano are the only two men my father has offered the reward to. Not as the *vaquero*, of course. But as the manhunters. With the *cuchillo* – the knife – instead of the gun. Garrido, he tells that he and Lozano are not skilled with the gun. With the knife, they would have beaten you – had you not been so quick with your *fusil* . . . your rifle.'

'It figures,' Steele growled, continuing to enjoy his supper as Flora Waldorf struggled up from the low sofa and came to the table.

'I wasn't friggin' armed and them guys couldn't have missed stickin' their friggin' stickers in me if I hadn't done what they told me!' Melvin Ivers slurred. And offered the bottle to the fat woman. Who took it and, like him, sucked the liquor from the neck.

'He tries to *salvar* – to salvage some pride, that is all,' Rosa said with a pitying glance toward the miserable Garrido. 'We Mexicans value such a thing.'

'It's what comes before a fall, Rosa,' Steele said, chewing and relishing the final piece of cold roast beef from his plate. 'And if they hadn't been so smart ass sure of themselves and used their fancy guns on me, maybe his buddy wouldn't have taken the worse kind of tumble there is. And this feller wouldn't have been left single handed.'

'You want me to tell him how to kill you next time, *gringo*?' Rosa asked bitterly, and deriving a brand of perverse satisfaction out of siding with another Mexican – albeit one on the other side in whatever conflict she was a part of.

'If the situation ever comes up again, I reckon he'll know, Rosa.'

'You want a drink, mister?' the fat woman asked, thrusting the bottle of rye at Steele. 'Wash down the grub?'

'He already said he don't drink hard liquor, Flora,' the saloonkeeper slurred.

'Cup of coffee would be good, ma'am.'

'I ain't so sure I oughta supply you and the woman with nothin' more until I seen the colour of your money, mister?'

Ivers was the kind of man who was permanently drunk and kept himself in a more or less constant state of contented inebriation by drinking steadily. While the fat woman who ran the boarding house needed just a few fast shots to alter from sober crotchetiness to drunken intransigence.

'Way this guy might've blasted me to Kingdom Come and didn't do it, Flora, he ain't gonna need to spend a cent in this town!' Ivers insisted, and the power of his steady if blood-shot-eyed gaze at the fat woman forced her to remain in docile silence as she rose to her feet and moved unsteadily out of the room to go fix the coffee.

'Where was I?' Rosa Canales asked rhetorically, angry at the interruption and demanding to be the centre of attention again.

'You were saying your father sent this feller and his partner looking for you with their fancy knives and promised them five – '

'To find me and bring me back home,' Rosa cut in, and her anger faded fast as the threat of tears gave her dark eyes a moist look in the light of the kerosene lamp hung from the ceiling over the table. 'And to kill Esteban if it was necessary.'

'Hey, that young feller that was with you last time you come through Curry was called Esteban, wasn't he?' Ivers muttered with a frown of perplexity on his fleshy face.

This as Flora Waldorf re-entered the room, carrying a coffee pot and two cups that she set down on the table. And said sourly: 'It must have been all of a week ago, Mel Ivers. I'm surprised you can remember that far back.'

Then she sat down beside him, snatched the bottle of rye from him, as he made to grab it back, snarled: 'Part payment of the tab you say you're gonna pick up for these people.'

The saloonkeeper blinked several times and shook his head vigorously, like he was trying to rid himself of some of the effects of his drinking. Then his mind fastened upon a memory of more recent origin than a week ago. And his voice was insistent as he said – swaying a little but able to keep his liquor-stained eyes fixed upon the Virginian's face: 'Wanna get my part told before I can't remember it, mister. Him and his *amigo*, they been in my place since they reached Curry. Couple of hours, maybe. One tequila apiece and then they sleep at the damn table. Customers like them I can do without. But I sure as hell wish they'd stayed sleepin'. When they woke up, they start to ask me questions about strangers that been through town. Easy to answer questions on account of we don't get many strangers through Curry. So I was able to tell the Mexicans that two of their kind were by here the other day. A young guy and his ladyfriend. Then, just as I was through tellin' them this, lo and behold, you and the little lady I was talkin' of come strollin' up the street.'

He paused, swaying still and needing to concentrate on what he was doing as he switched his gaze from the impassive face of Adam Steele to the etched with anxiety features of Gregario Garrido. Rosa Canales saw an opportunity to continue with her translation of Garrido's story, but remained in tight lipped silence after the Virginian shook his head as he pushed a brimful cup of coffee at her.

'His *amigo* was the boss. Did some fast talkin' in their lingo and then his *amigo* holds a knife in my gut while this one puts the friggin' gag on me and ties my hands behind my back. Just to keep me quiet and outta their way at first, I figure. Then the lamp's doused and the other guy goes up on the roof of my place.' He reached out blindly, was given the only quarter full bottle now, and took a swig. Sighed, and swept his gaze over every face as he concluded: 'Guess you all know the rest of it. When the other one gets his, this one gives me one hell of a bum's rush for the door. And I'm sure as shit figurin' I'm about to breathe my last. Did I thank you already for not blastin' away at me, mister?'

He was on the point of becoming the maudlin, ingratiatingly appreciative drunk as he peered across the table at Steele.

'Grateful for what you've told me, feller,' the Virginian answered. 'Which makes us even.'

Ivers punched himself in the centre of the chest and protested: 'My life is worth a hell of a lot more than that, mister!'

Then he took another swig from the bottle and abruptly passed out. One moment was sitting rigidly erect on the chair, then he rocked backwards and fell forward. And, with the smooth skill of long training, Flora Waldorf reached for the bottle and took it before it could fall from his loosened grip. While with her other arm she caught him by the scruff of the neck to break his fall and lower his head and chest gently to the table top.

'It ain't worth so much,' the fat woman allowed with a degree of tenderness in her voice and on her face as she looked at the drunken man. 'But there's worse folks than Mel Ivers around in this world.'

Garrido said something and Rosa translated: 'He wants to know what is going to happen to him?'

'Finish telling me what he told you, Rosa,' Steele instructed.

In response to the tacitly anxious query the injured Mexican directed at her, the woman shrugged her shoulders. Then frowned as she thought back to what she had been told and where she had got to before Ivers took over. Then:

'There is not very much more. My father allowed a week to pass before he sends these men after me. Perhaps hoping I will return of my own accord. Or perhaps taking the time to decide if he really wants me to return.'

'Garrido say that?' Steele asked as he finished the cup of coffee and poured himself another.

'No. He is just a hired killer, is he not? He would hardly – '

'Best you stick to the facts for now, Rosa.'

'*Seguro*. Okay. Garrido and Lozano have little difficulty in following us. And I think they do more of this kind of work than they do with the cattle. But he does not say this, either.

What happened in the *cantina* – the saloon of this man – you have heard. Of course, they know you are not Esteban Chevez. From a distance and in the dark, they could not tell if you were a Mexican. But they know what Esteban looks like from working with him at De Raza Hacienda. They think that maybe I am your prisoner. Or my new lover after I tire of Esteban.' She over-emphasised a grimace as she spoke this possibility. 'Or that my father has hired other searchers for me and you are such a man. Whichever is the truth, they cannot believe their good fortune in you bringing me to them here. And they think the easiest way to get me away from you is to kill you. *Loco hombres*! He tells that they are worried by the way you carry the rifle. But still they must *lucirse* . . . show what skill they have with the knives. And look what that got them?'

She stared scornfully at the wretched Garrido. Who managed to inject a degree of pride into his heavily pocked face as he rasped:

'*Punto de honra, Senorita Canales.*'

The woman's voice was as contemptuous as her expression when she snapped: 'A point of honour is what he says. He does not look so honourable now, uh? Less so for his – '

'Luck of the draw, Rosa,' Steele put in evenly. 'He lost a partner. I just lost a horse.'

'*Loco*!'

Flora Waldorf banged the now empty bottle down on the table top and complained: 'It's getting to be real late and seein' Mel Ivers sleepin' like a baby is startin' to make me realise how much rest I'm losin' since you people woke me up.'

'Your house so I reckon you can go to bed whenever you please, ma'am,' Steele told her.

'If you think I'm goin' to my bed with that murderer loose in my house!' she snarled, stabbing a shaking finger at Garrido.

'He won't be around to cause you any concern,' Steele

assured her – and drew a gasp from each of the women and a low groan of alarm from the black-clad mad when he reached down at the side of his chair and brought the Colt Hartford into view. And when he stood up and clicked back the hammer of the rifle, Garrido begged:

'*Senorita Canales, quiero hablarle* –'

'Holy Mother of God, you can't . . . ' Flora Waldorf gasped, suddenly sober.

'He wants to talk to you, Adam!' Rosa said.

The Virginian looked at each of them in turn as he canted the rifle to his shoulder, and expressed genuine surprise that what he had said and done had been misconstrued by the trio. And when he looked back at the black-clad, trembling man on the sofa he saw that Garrido had been so terrified he was to be shot down in cold blood that the crotch area of his pants had become darkly and damply stained. Then, as the acrid taint of urine permeated the already fetid with fear, body odour and bad breath atmosphere of the cramped dining room, Steele felt the final dregs of high tension drain out of him and was able to show a good humoured smile as he said:

'Tell him, Rosa.'

'Adam?'

'All I'm going to do is run him out of town. And I'm sorry I gave everyone the wrong idea.'

The fat woman was weak with relief that murder was not to be committed in her boarding house.

Rosa Canales gave a staccato voiced translation of what Steele had said and even before she was finished Garrido began to express his effusive gratitude and perhaps to offer obsequious apologies for his part in the trouble. But the Virginian cut in on incomprehensible Spanish to add:

'Tell him I'm sorry it made him wet his pants. It was never my intention to take the piss out of him.'

CHAPTER TEN

GREGARIO GARRIDO rode fast away from the town of Fort Curry. Heading out across the desert on the trail that stretched north-eastwards. Astride his own horse in his own saddle with all his own accoutrements. In the sheath and holster on his gunbelt was his own knife and his own bullet scarred but still serviceable Tranter revolver. He was not a rifleman.

He was in no mood or position to ask questions about what would become of the mount and gear of his late partner. Wanted only to be gone from this town – with just his life and his damaged pride if that was the way the taciturn American wanted it.

He had understood little of what Rosa Canales had said to Adam Steele while they were in the livery stable and the American said only enough to convey his orders – but he could guess from her tone and the scowl on her element ravaged face that she disagreed with giving him his freedom. Especially giving him back his knife and his gun as well. Then out on the street, when he was astride his black stallion and waiting for permission to leave, the woman had snapped a string of venom-dripping obscenities at him. Until a weeping fit choked back the words and she whirled to run across the street and into the boarding house.

Then Steele had said: 'All right, feller. Move on out.' And gestured with the rifle along the street toward the open trail beyond the town marker.

'*Muchas gracias, hombre,*' Garrido said with a hand raised

to touch the brim of his black hat. '*Buena fortuna. Otra vez, uh*?'

'I said to move on out,' Steele replied, and slapped his free hand down on the rump of the stallion.

Which set the animal to galloping fast down the slope of the street: at a pace his rider made no attempt to reduce even though he had control of his mount after just a few yards. Perhaps, the Virginian reflected absently as he moved off at an easy walk through the settling dust billowed up by the pumping hooves of the bolting stallion, because Garrido did not entirely trust him. And was eager to race out of effective rifle range in the fastest possible time. But, once the Mexican was beyond a point where even the most fortunate of handgun shots could find a vital target, Steele ignored the man on the galloping horse.

And when he halted under the town marker and slowly tracked his unblinking gaze over the vastness of the brightly moonlit desert to the north, the west and the east of Fort Curry it was for a sign of the presence out there of another lone rider that he searched – and did not find.

But, he wondered some thirty minutes later, did he hear something that indicated the mystery man was still around: albeit not close by? This while he soaked his naked body in a tub of cooling soapy water in his spartanly furnished and not too clean bedroom on the upper floor of Flora Waldorf's boarding house. Heard something, just as he was through carefully shaving the bristles off his blistered and peeling face, that sounded too much like a rifle shot to be anything else. Muted by great distance, but heard in the total isolation of the surrounding silence. From what direction the sound came it was not possible to tell. And so, with no supporting evidence upon which to build a theory while he lay on the narrow bed he shared with the Colt Hartford, the Virginian allowed his mind a free rein as he waited for sleep.

But when he woke at sun up the next morning, he could not even recall moving from the bathtub to the bed. So guessed that he had not needed any kind of soporific thought pattern to relax his exhausted body and wearied mind into sleep.

He was first awake in the boarding house and roused Rosa Canales by entering her bedroom and prodding her rear with the muzzle of the Colt Hartford. She returned to red-eyed awareness in a bad humour, but aside from the heaviness of lack of sleep and the sour scowl that both contributed to detracting from her good looks, she had obviously derived much from the night's peaceful rest with some fresh food in her belly. And the tub of hot water, of which she had made use before she went to bed, had also helped to get her back into good shape.

When he told her that Flora Waldorf and Melvin Ivers were both still sleeping off the effects of the bottle of rye whisky and that if she wanted breakfast – or at least coffee – before they left Fort Curry she would have to fix it, she snarled some rasping Spanish at him and dragged the bed-clothes up over her tousle haired head. But while he was across at the livery stable, preparing the burro and Miguel Lozano's stallion for a day's desert riding, he smelled woodsmoke in the bright, clear air of early morning – from closer at hand than the stack on the cookhouse at the fort. The smoke wisping from that chimney, and the two different uniformed men standing sentry duty on the walkway above the post gateway had been the only other signs of life visible in the community when he crossed the street from the boarding house to the stable. And later, when he led the two saddled animals back the way he had come, Flora Waldorf's kitchen chimney was the only one on the street that was smoking.

Steele was aware that he was being watched by the two cavalrymen guarding the entrance to the post – and also by somebody inside the boarding house. And after he had been sitting on the step of the house for perhaps two minutes, loosely holding the reins of the two animals, Rosa appeared in the hallway behind him. With a cup of strong smelling coffee in each hand.

'You prefer no breakfast, do you not?' she asked as she gave a cup to him.

'Right.'

'And are eager for us to be on our way, I think?'

'Yes.'

'I am slowly becoming familiar with rising early and going without the breakfast.'

There was a brand of contrition in her attitude. And a very female freshness about her appearance even though she wore the same clothes she had changed into after he freed her from the Apache braves. So she looked like she had bathed again, had certainly fixed her hair and done all she could to clean her shirt and pants, before she went to the kitchen to light the fire and start the coffee. And while she was doing this, she had also worked at improving her humour – so that she only made a face and did not snarl a matching retort when Steele answered:

'Yeah, Rosa. I reckon the richer you are, the harder real life hits you.'

He got up from his seat on the step and she emerged from the house, abruptly looking less attractive as the light of this morning's sun fell harshly across the scars left by the glaring heat of those of yesterday and before. And her mood worsened again after she had cast a bleak-eyed gaze along the empty street in both directions and then stared with a grimace at the two saddled animals.

'I will ride the burro and you the horse, I suppose?'

'I killed his owner, Rosa. There's a sort of code about such things that allows me to have his horse and other stuff without – '

'Esteban killed my burro at the river,' she cut in. 'Thus, this animal was his and it now belongs to you. Since you killed Esteban.'

Steele finished his coffee and took from a slender roll of

bills a five spot which he folded and creased so that it remained rigid when it was slotted through the handle of the cup. He put the cup down on the step of the open doorway and swung smoothly up into the saddle of the big stallion.

'It is too much,' the woman complained. 'For what little we had here. Just two of us.'

'The burro had shelter, feed and water as well, Rosa,' he reminded her. 'The burro that maybe wouldn't have been fit to ride if there was no – '

'*Esta bien*,' she interrupted wearily as she set down her cup beside the one with the money through the handle. Then, as she got astride the burro. 'It's okay. You are right again, Adam. But it is still too much.'

The Virginian was first to set his mount moving and the woman urged the burro to come close alongside the stallion.

'Funeral expenses to come out of it, too,' Steele added against the clop of slow moving hooves.

'The man who buries the corpse will have his clothing and perhaps some money he finds in the clothing. His gun and – '

'I didn't want any of that, so I didn't contribute any of it, Rosa.'

'Again it is the *punto de honra*, uh?' she said with a sneer of scorn. 'But you tell me this, *Senor Sincero* Steele – how you know the first person who finds the money does not keep it all himself. And maybe this person is not even one of those who is owed a part of it?'

'I know I've paid what I owe, Rosa,' he answered as they rode under the weathered town marker and on to the open trail. 'If the people it's due to can't protect what's theirs – '

'You're crazy, *gringo*. Full of crazy ideas. Crazy, also, to leave money when the keeper of the cantina says everything is on the house – *gratuito*.'

'Rosa?'

'*Si*?'

'We have a long way to go still.'

'I know this.'

'So if it's all the same to you, I'd rather you didn't keep talking all the while – just for the sake of talking.'

She looked angrily at him to demand: 'You think I am one of those women who is the *parlanchin*? The . . . how you say . . . *si*, the chatterbox? Who must hear the sound of her own voice all the time or she is not happy?'

'You haven't been that so far, Rosa.'

'Then what are you telling me, *gringo*?'

'That *I'd* be a whole lot happier if you kept quiet, Rosa. Either that, or get said what you really want to get off your chest.'

She shifted her gaze away from him to peer along the trail stretched out ahead of them, her mood changing from anger to sullenness. Said after several seconds: 'I do not understand what you say.'

'You're doing it again,' he answered and there was a degree of hardness in his tone.

'*Que*?'

The Virginian pursed his lips and blew out a stream of air with a soft sound that was not quite a whistle. Then: 'I reckon you do, young lady. But since we have so far to ride and it's going to take us a long time to get you home, I guess I can spare you a little of that time to spell it out for you.

'You, Rosa, it seems to me, are one scared *senorita*. Who is just itching to tell somebody what's troubling her. But I'm the only person available and you're not sure how I'll take what it is you need to say. So you're scared to tell me what has you so scared. And you're scared you may start blurting it all out and to hell with the consequences. So you try to keep your mouth busy with words that don't mean a damn thing to either of us while your mind works flat out at deciding whether to risk those consequences of me knowing what's bothering you.'

'I – '

'I'm not through, lady,' he said flatly as he looked at – and through – her as a feature in his field of vision while he was scanning the desert to the limit of the heat haze in the southeast. 'And the longer you listen to me, the less time you have to fill by your own efforts to keep the problem bottled up inside you. Not much longer, though. I just have to tell you that I'm certain you gave me an honest translation of what Garrido said last night.'

'*Ciertamente, Adam!*' she blurted and by the tone of her voice demanded that he look at her and see in her face that she was speaking the truth. '*Juraria que fue asi –*'

'Like I just told you, I'm certain of it, Rosa,' he said across her vehement Spanish. 'And, that being so, I know I'm in line to collect five thousand dollars when I deliver you to your father. So, unless what you're scared to tell me affects my chances of earning that money, Rosa, you have nothing to worry about by telling me.'

For a much longer time than before, the woman remained silent. And Steele had occasion to glance specifically at her with mild curiosity just once – when she shifted from her dejected attitude astride the burro. But this was just to turn and work free a blanket from the bedroll behind her saddle: and donned it, mantilla fashion again, to protect her head and shoulders from the glaring heat of the sun. And the Virginian returned to his effortless but systematic scanning of their surroundings – from which the last trace of the town of Fort Curry had now gone. And no sign of a lone rider, be it Gregario Garrido or another, was to be seen: unless in the confusion of tracks that marked the frequently used trail they were riding.

Then, perhaps fifteen minutes after she had withdrawn into her private world of dark reflections upon what Adam Steele had told her, Rosa Canales broke her silence.

'Adam?'

'Yeah, Rosa?' he answered, sounding disinterested as he did a double take at the far distance directly ahead of them.

But she was not conscious of anything so subtle as the tone of his voice as she continued to stare down at her own hands holding the reins of the burro – oblivious, also, to the stir of activity that maintained a hold on part of Steele's attention as she said:

'I am some rotten bitch, Adam. The worst person I know. Who deserves nothing good. Because I am so bad – so *malo*. So evil.'

She looked at him now, and was irritated to find him gazing ahead. Demanded: 'You are listening to me?'

'You hate yourself, Rosa,' he answered. 'I heard you say that without needing to look at you. The same as I didn't have to get out of the bathtub last night to hear a rifle shot a long way from town.'

Now she felt drawn to gaze in the same direction as Steele. And caught her breath at the sight of the disturbance some miles along the trail – a constantly moving patch of black on the pale colours of the desert, blurred by distance and the shimmering heat haze but unmistakably suggesting violence.

'What is it?'

'I reckon a bunch of buzzards. Doing what they have to do to survive, Rosa. But we'll know for sure in an hour or so. Guess you have more to tell me than that you hate yourself?'

Having been sidetracked from her purpose after taking so much time and effort to get started, the woman needed to compose herself again before she felt able to continue. And her unsettled state of mind was not improved by the compulsion she experienced to constantly glance at the squabbling, gorging scavengers.

'There are some who know of my situation who will tell you it is the fault of my father, Adam. And I am sometimes one of these. This depending upon how much of a rotten bitch I am at the time: how much of the hate I now feel for myself I direct toward him. You know what I am saying, Adam?'

'Nobody's unique, Rosa. We just all think we are sometimes – the worst of times, usually.'

'I start from the beginning, yes? He was a wonderful man

then, my father. My mother, she used to say he loved me better than he loved her. And better than De Raza Hacienda. That was the *broma* . . . the joke that was not quite the joke, Adam. My mother, as I remember her and as many who knew her better than me have told me, she understood my father's love for me and his wish to spend much time with me. But she had the much *resentimiento* . . . resentment, that he was a lot of the time doing the work of the hacienda. To become very rich and very powerful. For his own sake, I know, but also for me and for my mother to have the *goce* . . . the enjoyment.

'But my mother, she was impatient for the time when she and my father together would share the *fruto de su trabajo* . . . the success. And she leaves him. To go away with a *gringo*. A *frances* . . . a Frenchman from the Americano city of New Orleans. I was just . . . *cinco* . . . five years of age when this happens, so you understand why others I have spoken with knew my mother better than I?'

'Sure, Rosa,' Steele acknowledged, engaged in his usual three hundred and sixty degree surveillance again – paying no more attention to the gorging buzzards than he did to the pensively frowning, quietly talking woman riding the burro alongside him.

'After this has happened – my mother has gone to New Orleans with the *frances* – my father spends more time than ever with me. And, as I tell you before, I think, he sees that I have everything I desire. He spoils me is how you say it in your language. And when I am so young, it is not to be expected that I will try not to be indulged in this way, no?'

'You weren't unique at that age either, Rosa,' he allowed as he drank from one of his canteens. And, when she gave him a long, just vaguely sullen look, he added: 'I refilled both your canteens, too.'

'I do not think I could keep even water in my stomach until I am finished with this.'

'Just don't get dehydrated and pass out on me, Rosa.'

'*Si*,' she countered after a few moments of scowling thought. 'The *premio* posted by my father . . . the reward, it is not for me dead or alive.'

'You were saying you didn't kick against being spoiled when you were a child, Rosa.'

'*Si*. For then I am asked to do nothing in return. Not even to be good, for I am always forgiven. Just to show much love for my father.' She paused, frowned deeper and hurried on: 'Never the *abnormal* love, you must understand. My father loves me only as the *hija* . . . his daughter.'

'Okay,' the Virginian said when he glanced at her after she paused and found that she was staring fixedly at him – to stress the truth of what she had said and demanding that he confirm he accepted this.

'Loved me then and loves me now, Adam. Except that he demands more in return. Has made such demands since, as I think I told you earlier, about the time I became *dieciseis* . . . sixteen years old. And I begin to see that there should be other men interesting to me in addition to my father. And men other than he take the interest in me. Which is all perfectly natural, of course. And my father, he is understanding of this – for as long as there is no *seriedad* . . . no seriousness between the young men and me. For as long as – ' She began to chew on her lower lip as she spoke and there was something akin to shame in her dark eyes. ' – I treated them the way I acted toward my father, I suppose. I allowed them to spoil me in their ways and gave them nothing in return. Nothing but *angustia* . . . the heartbreak, anyway.'

She looked up from her hands, and a shudder shook her body. But it was not caused by vivid memories of how she had dashed youthful passions. Instead, they had ridden far enough up the trail now so that they could see the ugly birds clearly enough to pick out the splashes of crimson on their black plumage. This as the half dozen buzzards who had been at the feast moved sluggishly over the dark stained ground, scratching at and sometimes using their bills to investigate perhaps overlooked tidbits in the dust. All of them satiated, but in this hostile environment where the next meal might be days away, reluctant to move off before they were certain there was nothing more to be scavenged here. Their lumbering forms were between the skeletal remains of their meal and the approaching riders.

Rosa Canales took to staring fixedly down at her hands which toyed with the slack reins, as she continued with her story.

'Twice I had the taste of my own medicine and recovered, Adam. When I thought I had fallen in love with young men and then thought I would die after they left me. But to have a father like Don Benito was a great comfort. It certainly seemed so at the time. How was I to know that he was buying comfort for himself, too? Salving his *conciencia* . . . conscience with the *dinero que se paga por remordimientos* . . . the money for the conscience, you know?'

She was suddenly very embittered.

'Conscience money, Rosa,' Steele said. 'How did Don Benito get rid of the young fellers?'

'With the *dinero* . . . the money. That they accepted the *soborno* . . . the bribe means that neither was the kind of man I thought he was. Filipe was paid *dos mil* and Augustin accepted *tres mil.* Dollars American. *Canalla*! Scum!'

She shrieked the final few words, the sound of them resonant with hatred across the burning floor of the desert. And the buzzards were startled into sudden flight – awkward until the moment of take off, then becoming gradually more graceful as rising thermals of air reduced the amount of effort the birds had to apply to beating their wings. Until they were beautiful in soaring movement as they diminished in perspective against the blue glare of the sky. While below the birds the two riders closed the final few yards on the skeleton of a man, not quite picked clean: for there was dried blood and some hardened fragments of flesh and organs still clinging to bones here and there, the former crimson colour faded to dull brown by the harsh sun of half a morning.

Much of the man's clothing had been torn to shreds by the bills of the ravenous birds and it seemed that a good deal had been swallowed in the haste to gorge the fresh meat. But the metallic decoration had not been consumed. Nor the black hat, the gunbelt, the bullets in the loops and the Tranter with its elaborate etchings on the barrel. Nor the knife.

The revolver was still in the holster and the knife was in its sheath. But then neither would have been of any use to Gregorio Garrido against his attacker. Who had fired a rifle shot – Steele had heard and recognised the report for what it was – over a long range: at short range the bullet that had made just the one hole through the hat and the skull of the Mexican would have made others on the way out the other side.

'It is Garrido, is it not?' the woman asked, unable to look back at the skeleton after an initial glance, but even toned and apparently in no haste to leave the scene – if Steele wanted to stay.

'Right, Rosa,' he confirmed and heeled his horse forward, having scanned the surrounding area without dismounting. He had seen that the Mexican's stallion had bolted in the wake of losing his rider so violently – wheeled half to the left to race due south. Steele had failed to see any sign that the rifleman who had killed Garrido had ridden on to the trail to check on his victim.

'I cannot feel anything at his death,' the woman announced coldly as she moved her burro up alongside Steele's mount again. 'He was no better than the bounty hunter. You neither, I think?'

'I'm something like one of the buzzards about this thing, Rosa.'

'The *busardo*, Adam?'

'Not Garrido, Rosa. But if ever I get to meet up with the feller who killed Garrido, I reckon I'll have a bone to pick with him.'

CHAPTER ELEVEN

ROSA CANALES rode for more than a minute in pensive silence, frowning like she was trying to find the thread of the story she had been telling before the grisly interruption had sidetracked her. But the patiently waiting, horizon scanning Virginian was wrong to assume this was the reason for her thoughtful pause. And was surprised at the depth of feeling in her voice when she said abruptly:

'I swear to you, Adam, that I have not the slightest idea who this man is.'

He glanced into her blanket-shaded face and saw that the intensity of her expression, pleading to be believed, was a match for the tone of her voice.

'I don't doubt you, Rosa,' he assured her. 'So far I don't have any reason to disbelieve anything you've told me.'

'I thought when you spoke of the man in that way that you were . . . '

'He intrigues me, is all,' Steele said absently after she left the sentence unfinished. 'I was thinking aloud.'

She experienced a brief period of relief, then did have to take a little time to recall where she had got to before they rode up to the buzzard ravaged remains of the Mexican. Finally nodded and after a short lived grimace, took up the account.

'I find out about the *pagar y despedir* . . . the pay off to Filipe by accident. And in the big quarrel with my father over this, he tells me also how he gave the money to Augustin. I remain *furioso* . . . mad at my father for many days. Until I realise that something he has told me in the quarrel is correct.

That any man who has the choice of me or a few thousand dollars – even a million dollars – and takes the money, he is no kind of man for me. And I was lucky that my father discovered what kind of men Filipe and Augustin were.'

She pondered this point – obviously not for the first time – and after a short while she shrugged. Not entirely certain about the outcome but willing to stay with her father's view. Then she blinked several times, perhaps to rid her dark eyes of the threat of tears, and went on in a strong voice:

'For a long time, I offer no encouragement to any young men, Adam. Because of what has happened with those two, I am the *misantropo* . . . the hater of all men. For *cuatro* . . . for four years I am my father's little girl again. And I tell you, Adam, I have the greatest enjoyment – and I cost my father much money. Which he pays eagerly, since I know he feels bad about what he had to do to show me . . . '

Again she allowed a sentence to hang incomplete in the hot desert air. While her eyes glistened again, but not with latent tears. Instead with a smile that failed to touch her mouth line and might well have been malevolent. Then, seeing Steele suck from a canteen, she was shifted out of the reverie and needed to slake her own thirst.

'But then I meet Claudio Ruiz, Adam,' she went on, and spoke more quickly now, as if anxious to finish. 'He was the *viajante* . . . the travelling salesman for the *perfumeria* . . . the organisation that makes the *perfume* . . . this is the same, I think. And I cannot be the hater of this man, Adam.'

Just for a moment there was a glow of remembered joy in the sun-scarred face shaded by the mantilla-like blanket. Until an expression that was undoubtedly malevolent swept it away. And there was an acid tone in her voice.

'I thought I had taken the necessary steps so that my father did not know of my love for Claudio and his for me. And I admit, Adam, that I did this because I did not wish for this man to have the opportunity to choose between my father's money and his daughter. For I am certain it is true that every man has his price – and my father, he can afford to pay very high.'

She shrugged. 'But the man who has much money, he is able to use it in many ways to obtain and keep that which he wants, no? And I think that the secret of Claudio and I was sold to him by many people. But I have my spies on the De Raza Hacienda, too. Paid for with money I have only to ask for to be given. So I find out that Don Benito knows of Claudio and I. And I make the arrangements with Claudio for us to . . . to *fugarse.* To run away together . . . to elope, I think?'

'To run away to get married, Rosa?'

'*Si.*'

'To elope.'

'But Claudio does not meet me at the place we arrange. And it is from here, Adam, that I wish you to know for sure that I am telling the truth – that I lied at first because I did not want you to know what kind of an evil woman I am. For you might think I will make use of you – '

'Just tell it like it happened, Rosa,' Steele cut in, and again she felt compelled to look in the same direction he did when she glanced at him and saw that he was gazing fixedly ahead again. Saw the building that held his attention and supplied:

'It is the rest stop for the stage passengers, Adam. No longer used for that purpose for there are no more stagecoaches from Phoenix in this direction. Lately, it is used like the old church. For the soldiers on duty in the desert to rest.'

'Grateful to you,' the Virginian said. 'Reckon we should get there at about the right time to rest up around midday.'

'It will be welcome.'

'You know what happened to Claudio Ruiz, Rosa?'

There was no pause for gathering her thoughts this time. And it was like she was emotionally drained when she answered simply: 'My father killed him. Had him killed. Perhaps by Gregario Garrido. Or Miguel Lozano. Or any one of a hundred men like that who my father has surely used on many occasions to perform such tasks.'

'He decided he wanted you more than Canales money?'

'He was not given the choice.'

'Your father admitted to it?'

'I have not yet had the opportunity to ask him.' She shook her head vigorously and vented a low grunt of irritation. Angry at herself for dwelling on the past and needing to make a conscious effort to continue without prompting. '*Dispense usted.* I wait for very long time at the appointed place. Then a rider comes. I know it is not Claudio, for he does not ride. He drives the *carro* . . . the wagon in which he has the *mercancia* . . . the stock that he sells. I am afraid and I hide. Until Esteban announces it is he and he has bad news of Claudio.

'Esteban Chevez, he has been my admirer for some time. I know this. Since before Filipe and Augustin I knew of his feelings for me. And all the time I am the hater of men. During all these many years, he is *de ojos lunaticos* for me. I think you say in English, he moons for me.'

'I get the picture, Rosa.'

'*Bueno*. And during all this time, I treat him like my *hermano* . . . my brother. If I treat him kindly at all. Claudio, he knows of this, so it is to Esteban that he gives his trust. With his dying words.'

She curtailed what she was saying and for a long time the desert silence was disturbed only by the slow, clopping and creaking sounds of the horse and the burro moving along the trail. The animals carrying their riders closer to the one time stageline way station that Steele could now see was built of adobe and timber, sited in the vee of the fork where the Fort Curry spur angled off the main Phoenix to the Colorado River crossing trail.

When he looked at the woman, as a part of sweeping his gaze over the desert on his right, he was in time to see her brushing the silently spilled tears off her cheek. Before she jerked her face away from him and hurried on:

'Esteban was one of the hacienda workers ordered by my father to help with the ambush of Claudio as he drives his wagon to our meeting place. Much of the *perfume* that is in the wagon, it is made of a material that burns. The wagon is halted and it is burned. Claudio burns, too. My father orders this because he has the hatred of plotting against him. And he considers that in attempting to steal me, Claudio deserved the same punishment as if he had plotted to cheat De Raza Hacienda. You understand, Adam?'

'Sure, Rosa,' the Virginian replied, and now concentrated his unblinking gaze on the long, low building to the exclusion of all else. While his right hand moved off the reins to rest on his thigh, fingertips perhaps three inches from the jutting stock of the Colt Hartford in the forward hung boot. This as they rode to within a quarter mile of the way station at the meeting of the trails.

Rosa Canales was too involved in the past that she relived to be conscious of the high tension that had fastened a grip on the man riding at her side.

'Esteban was among those left to clear away the debris and conceal all signs of the murder of Claudio,' she went on bitterly. 'But Claudio was not quite dead when Esteban took him from the ashes. He recognised Esteban and told him where I was waiting. Implored him to come to me and warn me, for fear my father would also punish me for being party to the plot. Esteban did this for Claudio. And much more than this for me, Adam.'

Now she did become aware that, while he might well be hearing what she said, he was far more interested in the silent way station that showed many signs of neglect but was not in such a bad state of repair as the church several miles to the west.

'Adam, do you think – ' she began.

'He don't just think, girl!' a man growled from within the building. And laughed harshly when the horse and the burro were reined in some two hundred feet from the weather stained rear wall. 'And now you know the same as he does. Which ain't everything.'

'Reckon I know better than to try to get my rifle out of the boot, feller?' Steele said, his intonation adding the query, after Rosa Canales had gasped.

The barrel of the stranger's rifle was pushed into view now – out through one of the four windows in the rear wall. The hand that cupped the barrel at a midway point was also seen. But the deep shade of the roof at noon hid the rest of the cheerful sounding man.

'So you want to tell us the most important fact we don't know, feller?'

'How's that, mister?'

'What the *senorita* and I can do for you?'

The man at the window vented another short gust of harsh laughter. Then: 'You can go to hell, mister! So me and Rosa can spend some time in the other place, you know what I mean?'

The Virginian shot a sidelong glance at the woman when her name was spoken: and she caught the tacit query and expressed genuinely fearful ignorance of how the man in the adobe walled, timber roofed building knew who she was.

'If that's what she wants to do, I mean!' the stranger hurried on. 'Course, if she don't want to, I'll be real happy to just escort her home real polite like! Take her back to her Pa and take the reward money he's put up for her! Won't lay a finger on her if she don't wanna put out for me. But the way I hear tell, she just can't get enough of – '

'*Bastardo*!' Rosa shrieked. '*Soy* – '

A burst of rapid gunfire caused the woman to abruptly curtail her snarled retort to the insult she had interrupted. And then her mouth – still gaping wide to shout at the man in the former way station – began to vent a shrill scream of terror. That remained at the same pitch for as long as it counterpointed the fusillade of shots – and bullets cracked out of the glassless window where the stranger was positioned. These bullets not aimed at the man on the horse and the woman on the burro. For they had already found their target. And once free of the building descended through a short arc of decay to fall to the arid surface of the trail. While there spurted out in their wake over a lesser distance a spray of blood and even bloodied pieces of torn off flesh.

Perhaps five seconds passed while Rosa Canales screamed, six gunshots were fired, maybe five bullets dropped to the trail and an indeterminate quantity of human blood splashed into the dust. Before that silence which, it seems, is only ever so absolute in the desert, came to the world of the Mexican woman, the man from Virginia and the second stranger in the building with adobe walls and timber roof. A silence that lasted for a much shorter time – before the once threatening rifle clattered to the window sill, bounced and fell with a dull thud to the ground outside: and the corpse of the man who had been behind the threatening rifle toppled forward and folded double out of the window. His limp arms hanging and swinging, fingertips for a time brushing the stock of the Springfield single shot. Blood dripping down between the lax arms to be soaked up by the arid ground as eagerly as that which was sprayed while the man was being gunshot so mercilessly – coming out of the same gruesome head wounds that erupted what should have been another shrill scream from Rosa when she glimpsed the shattered face before the doubling over action across the window sill hid it.

But for stretched seconds, the woman's vocal chords refused to give sound to her new shock. And, in the silence she struggled to fill, somebody else made sounds.

A door opened.

A man snarled an inarticulate command.

A horse snorted.

There was a crack that, perhaps a half second after he heard it, Steele recognised as the slap of an open palm on horseflesh.

Then shod hooves hit hard packed ground as the man

drove his mount to an instant gallop.

East along the trail that stretched to Phoenix. The horse and rider racing into sight of the open mouthed Rosa Canales and the rigid in the saddle Adam Steele just a few moments after they first heard the crashing open of the door on the other side of the building.

And the woman rasped, the word just audible above the clatter of the pumping hooves: 'Claudio!'

'Appears he had no option but to leave it to you to fill me in on the rest of it, Rosa,' Steele said evenly against the diminishing sound of galloping hooves. And he left the Colt Hartford in the boot as he swung wearily out of the saddle. Then took hold of the bridle to lead the stallion toward the meeting of the trails.

'*Como*?' the still shocked Mexican woman asked huskily as she stared fixedly in the wake of the retreating horseman who was now all but lost amid the billowing dust of his mount's gallop. Then she shook herself free of whatever eerie sensation had a grip on her, recalled the Virginian did not understand her language and translated: 'What did you say, Adam?'

'Something like dead men tell no tales, Rosa,' he answered.

CHAPTER TWELVE

'I KNOW I make the mistake about Claudio, Adam,' Rosa Canales said disconsolately as she leaned against the wall and slowly slid down it until she was sitting on the floor at its base, knees raised and forehead resting on them.

This as the Virginian crossed from the door of the way station to the window where the dead man was slumped over the sill – and used the Colt Hartford as a lever to tip the corpse on to the outside. Then he re-crossed the room that still smelled of exploded powder and the sweat of men and a horse and told the woman as he went out:

'It's lunchtime, Rosa. You want to fix us something?'

'*Donde esta* . . . where are you going?' she demanded, suddenly afraid again, as she scrambled to her feet and swung out of the doorway and on to the derelict stoop behind him.

'This isn't walking country,' Steele answered as he moved along the front of the one-time way station. 'Should be another horse up for grabs, I figure. Or another burro, maybe.'

'*Bueno*,' she said absently as she turned to their two mounts which were hitched to the section of stoop rail still in place. Recovering from shock, but still with a strange mixture of incredulity and yearning in her dark eyes as she lifted down the saddlebags and canteens but directed her attention along the trail that stretched eastward. A trail that was as empty and silent as the flanking desert now, the elegantly garbed rider having galloped from sight and out of earshot while she and the Virginian covered the final few yards to reach the way station. She too shaken to trust herself to speak and he devoting his entire attention to the now totally silent building – obviously not trusting its death-featured serenity.

And Steele sweated still and maintained a tighter than usual one-handed grip on his rifle as he moved cautiously toward the second door in the front of the weather-stained, adobe-walled building. Passing three windows, but all of them with closed shutters. Then, through cracks in the warped timbers of the shutters on the final window he passed came a smell of animal much stronger than that which permeated the air back in the room where murder had been committed.

The second doorway was higher and wider than the first – designed for horses to pass through. Gave access, once the creaking door was swung outward, to a stable where stage teams had been rested in the old days. This day in the stable that was as lacking in equine comforts as was the room in facilities for human travellers there was just the one horse. A living animal but in most other respects having a great deal in common with his former owner.

He was a stallion of fairly advanced age, with a dark coat dappled with grey, shaggy and matted with sweat crusted dust. Weary and dejected. Laden with an ancient saddle and accoutrements that were as ill cared for as the animal. There was an adequate supply of water in the canteens for a day or so for horse and rider. Enough preserved food in the saddle-bags to keep a man reasonably well fed for a week. There was nothing on or about the animal to give any clue to the identity or character of his owner beyond the obvious fact that the man cared little for the welfare of his mount.

'The food is ready for eating, Adam!' the woman yelled as Steele ran a comforting hand down the nose of the horse: this after he had checked that the animal was well enough shod and had no visible sign of injury or disease.

Now unhitched the reins and led the docile stallion out of the stable. To place him alongside the other horse and the burro in the early afternoon shade of the north facing building.

'I am not so hungry,' the woman said, waving a hand over the spread blanket on which she had laid out two cups of water and two plates meagrely scattered with some strips of jerked beef, some broken hard tack biscuits and a heap of cold beans. His plate contained perhaps twice the amounts she had given herself.

Steele nodded and absently fingered through the fabric of his reach-me-down shirt the scar tissue of the bullet wound in his upper right chest as he lowered into a cross-legged attitude in front of his meal. Said:

'I don't recall it, but I reckon I lost my appetite the only time I thought I saw a ghost, Rosa. But it was definitely dead.'

She sighed and shook her head slowly. 'It was the way he was dressed, Adam. He had the build that was similar, but many men I have seen since the *asesinato* of Claudio . . . since he was murdered, have been similar to him in such a way. But not since I came with Esteban away from the *vecindad* . . . the area of De Raza Hacienda have I seen anybody who is dressed with such *elegancia*.' She sighed again, and gazed into the middle distance as she went on. 'At home, when the work of the day was done, everybody who comes to the house must have on the clean clothes. And be clean themselves.'

She realised abruptly that she was speaking aloud the kind of wishful thoughts she had indulged when she gazed after the rider who had gone from sight. Glanced with a hint of embarrassment at the Virginian, and discovered that he, too, seemed to be lost in thoughts that had little bearing on the here and now – if the oddly empty expression on his heavily bristled, sweat beaded face meant anything.

In fact, his mind had remained only briefly in that part of his memory where were stored the events leading up to his getting shot. And now as he ate the spartan meal and listened with half an ear to what Rosa Canales was saying, he reflected upon what had seemed to be such an irrational fear he experienced in the wake of the unknown man being so violently shot to death. And, just a moment after she paused to look at him, reached the conclusion that it was not as irrational as he had initially considered it to be. It was simply an apprehensive respect for an element in this violent episode that he did not understand.

The mystery rider in the muted toned but unquestionably dudish outfit was no longer some phantasmagorical figure that came and went on the outer limits of actual existence. Momentarily glimpsed at such a distance that a man could not be entirely certain he had seen anything – until sign in the dust proved he had. Maybe heard in the cold and dark night – in the form of a far off crack of a rifle shot. With the picked clean bones of the victim to provide the proof. When not briefly in sight or within earshot, the presence of the mystery rider sensed by the Virginian who set such store by his ability to feel when he was under surveillance.

But now the man had been seen at close quarters. In the immediate wake of yet another incident which appeared staged to show that he meant no harm to Adam Steele and Rosa Canales. Yet, at the same time, was carried out in such a way that the man was taunting the couple with the fact that he had the undoubted capability to harm them if it suited him.

And the Virginian could think of no reason why the man should need to convey this – short of sheer arrogant pride or, and this factor was the cause of his healthy concern, a desire to prove himself better than the man who at the moment had five thousand dollars worth of woman in his safe keeping. Prove himself for as long as it pleased him to do so, until he tired of the cat and mouse game or the time for the money to be paid came close. When he would . . .

Goddamnit, the mystery man had to be an old enemy of Adam Steele. He even mocked him in the style of his garb – attired in the kind of high-priced, high-class tailored clothing that at the best of times was favoured by the Virginian.

Rosa Canales caught her breath and even flinched in her

cross-legged posture on the floor when the vacant look was abruptly swept from the face of the man opposite her by a scowl of evil rage. But then Steele regained his composure – and was impassive again on the outside as he held in check the white heat of temper that in years gone by had proved uncontrollable.

'Adam, I am sorry if – ' the woman began.

'You didn't do anything, Rosa,' he cut in on her evenly as he doused the final flames of a fury that would have been as illogical as his trepidation had been a few minutes earlier. 'Be grateful if you tell the rest of it.'

'I swear I know nothing of the man who did – '

'Esteban Chevez, Rosa. What happened after he told you Claudio Ruiz was dead?'

'*Si* . . . yes. It is nearly all told now, Adam,' she answered quickly, pleased that she had not caused his anger and eager to do what he asked so that he would not direct his perhaps still volatile ill-humour at her. 'I am devastated by what he tells me. *Inconsolable* . . . you say much the same I think?'

She paused for him to reply, he said nothing as he swallowed some food and she shrugged before she continued: 'But I know Claudio is in error in fearing that my father will do bad things to me. And Esteban, he knows this, too. He tell me this. But he also tells me I should go away with him. As I had planned with Claudio to leave De Raza Hacienda. Not to become the *matrimonio* . . . not to be the husband and wife. Esteban, he knows I do not love him as I loved Claudio. But he is ready to risk the murderous anger of my father. To take me away and hope that perhaps my *compasivo* . . . my feeling for him will change.

'And this is what I do, Adam. My *aborrecimiento* . . . my *odio* . . . the way I have hatred for my father on that night – I agree to leave with Esteban. And it is as I tell you before. We have just the one horse that is Esteban's and we have *poco dinero* . . . not much money. And at the town of Phoenix the money it runs out, and we have to sell the horse and some other things to buy the burros and are cheated – '

Steele uncrossed his legs and got to his feet, shaking his head as he rose. Until Rosa Canales became aware of his negative gestures and tilted back her head to peer questioningly up at him, genuinely concerned again about what she could have said or done wrong.

'Adam?' she posed, so obviously genuine in her puzzlement that he believed her.

'No, Rosa,' he said evenly as he swung up a leg and eased smoothly out of the window with the blood spattered sill. And, once standing outside the building, looked squarely at her so that she was able to see his expression matched his tone when he augmented: 'I reckon you think that's what you told me before. But what you said was that Esteban was your true love. You planned to run off with him. Your father had him beaten up and you had to leave home without him. You had arrangements to meet up in San Fran – '

'*Dios*!' she exclaimed. 'Adam, I – '

'Sure, Rosa, you had a good reason, I reckon,' he cut in. And ducked down out of her sight to check over the dead man as thoroughly as he had examined his horse.

'Now I remember,' she continued after a pause of several seconds. 'In my mind I am mixing up the truth with what I feel I must tell you at first. I was very much *asustado* . . . very frightened after you free me from the savages. I tell the complete truth now and I think you will understand?'

'Whichever way you want to tell it, Rosa,' he said into the pause that followed her obvious request, while he worked methodically and with no display of squeamishness at searching the clothing of the corpse – that was already beginning to smell cloyingly sweet in the desert heat.

'Esteban and I, we travel together on the same horse. From De Raza Hacienda to Phoenix. This is true. And from Phoenix to the Rio Colorado we ride the burros for which we have paid too much money. For much of the time, we avoid going into the towns. For we know my father will search for us. And the fewer people who see us, there are less to tell him or his men in which way we are going.

'To Phoenix we had to go. And to the town of Fort Curry after we reach this place where we are now. Or else we starve or we die of the thirst. You find out anything, Adam?'

Steele had come erect, into her sight again, and now re-entered the former way station. Told the woman: 'Seems his name was Erskine Lomax and he's got a brother back in Topeka Kansas who wrote to him in Sante Fe New Mexico. He doesn't have a cent on him. Fifty-five years old, maybe. Who didn't do anything with his life – or if he did, it doesn't show to me. Reckon he was just passing through and resting up here when he got caught up in somebody else's business.'

'Much as you were passing through a place when you became *meterse en* the business not of your making, Adam?'

'I'm still alive and hopeful of collecting five thousand dollars, Rosa,' Steele answered as he gestured for her to pack up the gear they had used during the meal. 'He's had half his head shot away and if he was promised money instead of threatened with a gun, I reckon it was a lot less than that. You put the bullet in Esteban's belly at the river crossing, Rosa?'

She had begun to do as he asked, already taking care to be neat with the chore. But now she pointedly kept her head bent so that she avoided meeting his steady gaze. And swallowed hard before she replied:

'I swear to tell the truth, and so I tell it, Adam. For long time – since before we reach Fort Curry. Perhaps back to Phoenix, when the money becomes less and the travelling is hard, we both have the *pensandolo* . . . how you say – the second thoughts, no?'

'Yeah, Rosa.'

'*Si.* I now realise it was the mistake to leave with Esteban. And Esteban, he comes to see me as a woman to . . . *codiciar* . . . as with the savages . . . for the expending of the lust, you know?'

'I see, Rosa,' Steele told her, and ushered her out of the

way station, taking the cups from her. 'And when you were camped somewhere close to the river crossing, he made a pass at you? That means he tried to scr . . .'

'I know what it means. And yes, you are correct. Esteban attempted to do as the savages would have done had you not prevented it, Adam. But I was not the prisoner as they made me. First I try to tell him to leave me be. To take me back to my home and I will tell my father he has found me and . . .' She shrugged as she broke off and watched Steele place most of their gear on the back of the burro. 'He would not listen. So I get his rifle and I warn him. But he does not believe I will shoot him. So I shoot him.'

He completed the transfer of equipment and signalled that Rosa should mount the neglected stallion of the dead Erskine Lomax. Then, with the reins of the burro in one hand, he swung up into the saddle on the horse of another dead man.

'You knew he wasn't dead, Rosa?'

He asked this over his shoulder as he heeled the better horse into movement, leading the burro. She quickly mounted the other stallion and then was cautious with her new ride as she urged him up alongside that of Steele. Only then answered:

'I did not know nor care. He had been like an animal as he tried to mate with me. I knew just that he was unable to try to prevent me from leaving him. With San Francisco as my *destino* . . . my destination. Hating Esteban more now than I had hated my father.'

She had been spitting out the words venomously as she relived the experience of shooting Esteban Chevez with his own rifle. But now she moderated her tone and showed an expression of deep remorse before she donned the blanket, mantilla like again, to throw a shadow over her face.

'It was my *intencion* to go to the city of San Francisco and to remain there for as long as I was able. Before I communicate with my father . . . send him the message. After he has had much time to be anxious for me. Which was very *estupido* of me, no? With just the two burros and a few dollars? And no *experiencia* of such country as I must cross. Except when I am safe in the hunting party with my father.'

She sighed and shrugged. 'And so I am made captive by the savages. I am lucky they do not kill me right away. Or have their way with me and then kill me. More lucky when you are my *salvador* . . . you save me. And now I am *avergonzado* . . . I feel shamed by the *mentiroso* I am . . . *maldita sea*! I am ashamed of the lies I tell you to make you want to help me.'

'Your father really is rich, Rosa?' the Virginian asked evenly.

'*Si*, perhaps the richest man in all of Chihuahua!'

'And it wasn't horseshit you told me – that your father's put up five thousand dollars for your safe return?'

'It is what Gregario Garrido told me, I swear it,' she assured him earnestly.

'So let's get the lead out, Rosa.'

'Adam, I do not underst – '

'Sooner we get you home the better?'

'*Si*, but – '

'And I reckon it's true that a fool and his money are soon parted.'

CHAPTER THIRTEEN

ROSA CANALES made to urge her mistreated horse to a faster pace, then realised Steele had no intention of making better time. At first was puzzled as she reflected that she may have misunderstood him. Then she glimpsed the trace of a fleeting smile on his profile and recalled in a different frame of mind their final exchange. And scowled as she demanded:

'You make another joke, *gringo*?'

'Did I?' he answered, not interrupting his routine watch on their surroundings.

'*A expensa de mi padre* . . . at the expense of my father?'

'If he's so rich, he can afford a little expense, I – '

'I wish no more to discuss anything with you if you cannot be *cortes* . . . be civil about . . . '

'That's fine with me, Rosa,' he told her evenly. 'I'm happy I know enough.'

And for a long time – perhaps more than an hour – they rode through the desert heat of the afternoon without a word passing between them. While Steele watched for a movement on the encircling horizon blurred by the shimmering heat haze, and the woman stared straight ahead. He with a mind that was open to admit any line of thought and was host to none: she obviously concentrating very hard – on one line, on many or maybe at barring all.

Then Steele signalled a halt so that he could dismount and move off the trail to a clump of stunted mesquite. Enclosed in her private world of deep thought – or its opposite – Rosa Canales was once more puzzled. But then, when Steele halted and, only partially hidden by the mesquite, obviously urinated, she vented an unladylike grunt of comprehension. And, when the Virginian was back in his saddle and they were moving once more at an energy conserving walk, the woman uttered a similar, but louder sound.

'You want to say something, Rosa?' he asked.

He glanced directly at her and saw that she compressed her lips – as if to emphasise that she intended to keep them sealed. But a half minute later, she changed her mind.

'I think that you have said my father is a fool.'

'I did?'

'For offering to pay money to have his *punetera* of a daughter back.'

'*Punetera* mean what I think it does. Rosa?'

'Bitch! It means the bitch.'

Steele nodded, like he was acknowledging her reply to his direct question. But then said: 'If it's what you think you are, maybe you can start doing something to change it.'

'And live happily ever after, *gringo*?' she suggested scornfully.

Now the Virginian shook his head and, at the completion of the gesture, peered fixedly along the arrow-straight trail. While he said, absently: 'That only happens in stories, Rosa. There never are any happy endings in real life. Because everybody who lives has to die in the end. And there's nothing happy about dying.'

'Claudio and I would have had much happiness before we . . . ' She recognised the change that had come over Adam Steele and broke off to peer eastward, too. But failed to see anything different about the arid, sparsely featured terrain from when she had last looked across its parched surface – albeit with a total lack of interest in the vista. 'There is new danger?' she demanded, looking at his unmoving profile now: her anger at him of a few moments ago washed away by a surge of fear.

'Maybe, or maybe not. Which means I don't have any

idea. Which is a waste of words. But they're plentiful enough, even out in the desert.'

He began to rake his gaze in other directions now and after a few moments most of the woman's tension drained out of her. But she saw that he paid most attention to the horizon immediately ahead of them. And she maintained a careful watch to the east, too. Said, after a brief pause:

'I think perhaps, you tell me that I am wasting the words if I try to make the excuses for what I am?'

'You don't have to make excuses to me, Rosa. Far as I'm concerned, you've said enough. Reckon that's what I was trying to say when – '

'Adam!'

'Now there's something you don't see plenty of in the desert,' he continued, speaking in the same easy tone as before she shrilled his name. The woman seeing, as did he, the momentary flash of reflected daylight. 'Nature never did put anything in the desert that glints like that. Ring any bells?'

'*Que*?'

Steele narrowed his eyes, struggling to see into the distant heat haze and confirm what he thought he had seen. And he did not respond to her counter query for perhaps two minutes. By which time they had covered enough ground for the range of low ridges to show clearly.

'Some hills where the trail came out on to this stretch of desert, Rosa. Best part of a day's ride from the way station where you and Chevez headed down the spur toward Fort Curry.'

She nodded several times while he was speaking and was quick to supply as he finished: '*Si, me mal no me acuerdo* . . . if I remember correctly, Adam, they are called the Gila Bend Mountains. Esteban and I were told – '

'Fine, Rosa. When you and he came out of the hills, did you pass through a town or by a house, another way station . . . anything like that? With glass windows?'

There was another glint of sunlight reflected off a man-made object as he finished the question. And she gasped and needed to swallow hard before she could reply:

'No, nothing. Not in those mountains. On the trail. You think . . . ?'

'I know.'

'What is causing it?'

'No, Rosa.'

'But you said . . . '

'I know that worrying about what's causing it won't serve any purpose.'

'That is easy to say.' She dragged her gaze away from the line of hills that now showed dark and clear against the heat shimmer. But felt drawn to look back at them, and shuddered as she added 'But much harder to do.'

There was just one more glint of reflected sunlight, seen to be in direct line with where the trail ran off the desert and into the hills. Then the slopes and ridges of the Gila Bend Mountains became as impassively uncommunicative as the face of Adam Steele. Movement there was on the features of the man as he breathed and as an occasional bead of sweat squeezed from a pore and coursed across his bristled skin. And movement there appeared to be among the hills – as shadows changed shape and direction almost imperceptibly to the dictates of the dipping sun.

Then evening came and quickly gave way to night, the dusk and then the darkness settling over the more easterly high ground some time before they dropped over the two riders and their three animals. And when full night with its bright moon blanketed the entire terrain, Rosa Canales once more brought a long talk-free silence to an end. Abandoned her surveillance of the hills that were still some three miles distant and sighed with relief before saying:

'You know what I think it was, Adam?'

'No.'

'The man at the way station. He has something that has

been much polished. On his clothes, perhaps. Or his gun, it could be. He is riding away from us still, and this is why we see the *llamarada* . . . the flash of the sunlight on this thing so few times. He has gone too far into the hills and is out of the sun to us. You think this could be so, Adam?'

'Sure it could be, Rosa.'

'If I think this is so, then I do not have the worry.'

'I told you not to do that, a long time ago.'

'*Si*, Adam. But when you first tell me this, I am still confused by what has happened at the place where the *gringo* . . . the man called Lomax is shot. But I have thought much of this. I have thought that if the man who killed him meant to harm us, he would have done so there, no?'

'Right, Rosa.'

'So I think it was the man Lomax who meant harm to . . . to you. So that he could have me to himself to take to my father and get the five thousand dollars.'

'Could be, Rosa.'

She smiled, enjoying his agreement with so much of what she was saying. Hurried on: 'And so we really have no reason to be worried by him, Adam. He is on *nuestro equipo* . . . on our side. He is our *compadre.* Did he not also kill Gregario Garrido who also meant you harm, Adam? So a *companero de armas* . . . a companion in arms to us. Almost the *angel de la guarda* . . . the guard . . . '

'Sure, Rosa,' Steele said. 'All that is why I'm not worried about that feller, either. Yet.'

'*Todavia*?' she asked, snapping her head around to stare at him, her new found peace of mind suddenly eroded. 'Why will it be necessary to concern yourself with him later?'

'Angels have wings for high flying, Rosa,' he answered, and continued to peer at the point where the trail went into the hills.

'Adam, if you are again making the – '

'We've already seen he has an expensive taste in clothes. Maybe his harp needs some new strings. Five thousand dollars will buy a lot of catgut, I reckon.'

She was suddenly looking at him aghast and there was a strangled tone to her voice when she forced out: 'You mean you think he is waiting until we are almost at De Raza Hacienda – then he will . . . '

Steele, with a pursing of his lips the only change of expression, suddenly reined his horse to a halt. And let go of the leadline by which he had led the burro. Then had the Colt Hartford out of the boot a second later when the woman had stopped her mount. For another second she continued to gaze across at his profile in deep surprise becoming fear after she had curtailed what she was saying. Only then realised she had to look elsewhere to discover the reason for the abrupt interruption to the night ride. Blurted, in an even more choked tone:

'*Dios, mi padre*!'

She made to urge her horse into a lunging gallop: then stared back at the Virginian with a mixture of anger and pleading when he shot out his free hand, to grasp her reins and wrench them from her.

'Easy, Rosa,' he rasped softly. 'Speaking of your father, I don't think we should rush in where maybe even a guardian angel fears to tread.'

CHAPTER FOURTEEN

FOR SEVERAL stretched seconds, high tension kept the woman mute while her mouth opened and closed as she constantly wrenched her head from side to side – staring with unblinking eyes from Steele to the point where the trail emerged from the shadowed hills and back again. Was finally able to force out:

'*De coche de dos caballos*, Adam! The carriage and pair of my father! I would know them anywhere, I tell you! They are famous wherever he goes. If you do not allow me to go to him so that I may explain who you are, he will perhaps think that you . . . '

Her voice was just beginning to sound almost normal in tone when she found herself forced to abandon her plea – while she stared fixedly now along the trail to where a two-horse team was pulling a four-wheel buggy at an easy trot over the moon-bright way between the hills and where she and the Virginian waited.

The buggy was a spider phaeton with highly polished bodywork and a great deal of silver trim. The horses which drew the carriage were snow white in colour, held in harness that also had a high sheen and was decorated with silverwork. The front seat canopy was folded down so that the man who drove the rig could be seen by Rosa Canales and Adam Steele. And they could also see a passenger who stood on the footboard of the phaeton's rumble seat immediately in back of the driver. And a black horse with a saddle on its back that was hitched to the rear of the rig.

The entire smoothly moving tableau was seen only in terms of varying shades of darkness relieved by the pure white of the team horses and the glinting silver of the decoration for what seemed a long time. And it was during this period – while the rig rolled to within five hundred feet of where she was forced by Steele to wait – that the woman sensed her excitement was misplaced.

The Virginian, too, felt a foreboding as he constantly altered the focus of his eyes to see clearly the moving rig and the dormant hills behind. And, side by side with this sensation of impending violence, he also felt ominously impotent: although certainly a part of what was happening, somehow detached from it and with no positive role to play. Felt this to such an extent that after he had withdrawn his hand, releasing the reins of the woman's horse, he did not move the Colt Hartford to the aim and thumb back the hammer. Instead, slid the rifle back into the boot as he warned Rosa in an even tone:

'You don't start to breathe again soon, you'll pass out.'

She sucked in some of the cold air of the desert night and rasped softly: 'Something *horroroso* is happening here. It is like the *pesadilla* . . . the bad dream from which I awake with screams. But I am already awake.'

'Sure, Rosa. I reckon I'm on my way out of a five thousand dollar dream.'

The pumping of hooves on the trail, the rolling of wheelrims, the creak of springs and the jingle of the metalwork on the harness gradually rose in volume. Then fell in cadence as the trot was slowed to an easy walk.

'He holds the gun to the head of my father,' Rosa Canales said dully, incapable of deeper shock as the phaeton rolled close enough for more than mere shapes and shades to be seen. And ominous feelings were confirmed by substantiated facts.

The man in the driving seat was a male version of Rosa Canales who had lived more than twice as long as her. And had lived a lot better if first impressions were given credence. For Don Benito looked in good shape, despite being under threat of having a bullet blasted into his head. He was a match for his daughter's five and a half feet height and, like her, carried little excess weight. His hair was grey instead of black and was a great deal thinner than Rosa's. Just as his handsome face had the same basic structure but was stretched over with skin that showed more of the scars left by passing time. But then Don Benito was close to sixty years of age. His clothing was as elegant and as well cared for as the horses he drove and the carriage he rode in – like he had only just come off his hacienda.

'He doesn't look like he's driven up here from Chihuahua, Rosa,' the Virginian drawled.

'He would not have done so alone. Always when he travels he has the *sequito* . . . you say, I think, the entourage?' She shrugged and Steele had the impression she was in the grip of the same kind of disassociated sensation as was he. 'The servants to attend to the *mantenimiento* of the standards. And, of course, the *guardaes-paldas*. The bodyguard.'

She continued to gaze apathetically at the rig as it came to a halt when the horses in the traces were some twenty feet or so away from those with riders in the saddles. While Steele, the feeling of passive indifference strengthening its grip on him, glanced once more toward the dark hills. Just mildly curious about the missing men.

'Rosa, it is good to see you again,' Don Benito Canales greeted as he applied the brakes of the phaeton, his voice as calm as his attitude.

'*Padre, que esta haciendo* – '

Don Benito Canales held up one white gloved hand to silence his daughter and asked of Steele: 'You speak our language, *senor*?'

'No, I don't,' the Virginian replied, concentrating his attention over the left shoulder of Canales at the man who stood behind him. A man just briefly glimpsed as he galloped his mount east from the one time way station: and before that seen as just a distant speck against the Mule Mountains of southern California. Between those occasions, heard once when he killed a man in the dead of night: and thought about a great deal. Finally seen clearly in the bright moonlight at close quarters.

A Mexican. Perhaps as old as Don Benito Canales. But taller and broader; stronger looking. And with more strength of character, too, in the shape and texture of his face. Dressed, as Steele had judged back at the way station, in the manner which he himself preferred. Except that the Virginian liked the hues to be a little brighter.

'Then we will say what has to be said in your language,' Canales said and there still was nothing in his demeanour to reveal he was concerned at having the muzzle of a small six-shooter pressed to the side of his head, just under his left ear.

'Papa, what are you doing here like this? Who is this man? Where are your men who always – '

Rosa had obviously shaken free of the lethargy of unreality for there was a shrill urgency in her tone now.

'In the order you asked the questions, *senorita*,' the man with the threatening gun cut in on her. 'He is here to see you die.'

Rosa caught her breath . . .

'My name is Eduardo Riaz and from this you will correctly draw the conclusion that I am related to Claudio. In fact, his father.'

The woman vented a strangled, very short scream . . .

'Your father's employees are waiting in the hills behind us. For his safe return – provided he does nothing foolish. And your American companion continues to show the good sense he displayed when he replaced his rifle in its scabbard. Having doubtless realised that none of this is of concern to him? Realised with a certain amount of relief, I would hazard a guess? Having seen the extent to which he is outclassed?'

Riaz was smiling when he started his replies to Rosa's questions. But the expression developed into a contemptuous sneer as he voiced the boastful taunts to Steele. Who, listening to the arrogant Mexican and almost feeling the scorn in his eyes touching him while he was being scrutinised from head to toe, was suddenly triggered out of detached indifference – and had to make an effort to prevent this from showing.

He said evenly: 'You've been good, feller.'

The smile was re-established. 'I was the best. When I was younger and harder. I led the most feared bandit group in the whole of Mexico. The best at what is necessary to be such a man outside the law, *gringo.* And the smartest to know when there is enough money to become respectable.'

'*No le comprendo* . . . I do not understand what is happening?' Rose Canales asked of her father who sat in seemingly effortless composure while the self-praising Riaz kept the gun muzzle pressed hard against his head.

'Your lover would hardly be pleased to tell you his father – '

'*Callarse, hijo de puta*! You are not the boss here!' He ignored Steele now, to stare levelly at Rosa Canales. 'So you do not understand, *senorita*? Then I will explain it all to you. Because I have the far greater *compasion* than your father had for my son, Claudio.

'I am like your father in other ways though, nowadays. The businessman. I manufacture the perfumes and Claudio is one of the many who sells the Riaz merchandise to the stores. But when I hear of what Don Benito Canales has done to Claudio – because he does not think he is good enough for you, *senorita* – I abandon my respectable business to return to what I did before.

'At first I think I will simply kill Don Benito Canales. But this, I decide, will be too easy for him. Much more satisfactory, I think, to take from him what he has taken from me. His only child.'

Rosa uttered a gasp that drew a bitter smile from Riaz and brought a change over the face of her father for the first time – he showed an expression of utter desolation that made him look suddenly twenty years older.

Steele shifted slightly in his saddle and Riaz displayed his high degree of alertness when he looked at the Virginian and snapped:

'To guard against the accident, *gringo*, I think it best you take the rifle from its scabbard and throw it to the ground.'

Steele did not quite follow the Mexican's instructions to the letter. After he had eased the Colt Hartford from the boot – gripping it over the end of the stock – he leaned far down to the side to lower it rather than throw it to the trail.

Riaz grunted his satisfaction when this was done and returned his gaze, his eyes smiling again, to Rosa. 'But first I must find you, *senorita.* For I learn that you are perhaps as heartbroken as I over – but no, you have quickly found another man to take you away – '

'*Haga el favor de* – '

'*Callarse, ramara*!' Riaz snarled, and the smile was swept aside by a scowl. 'If you listen, you will understand. I learn you have left De Raza Hacienda with the man who replaces my dead son in your affections . . . '

He intensified his glowering scowl at Rosa, challenging her to take issue with what he said. While her father, aware of more force applied to the threatening gun where it pressed against his flesh, transmitted a tacit plea for her to remain silent; then moved his eyes along their sockets to start to send a plea of a different sort – only to abandon it as useless with a change of expression that came close to suggesting scorn at sight of the ill-clothed, travel-stained and seemingly helplessly unarmed Adam Steele.

'And then I realise,' Eduardo Riaz went on, expressing pleasure at his control over his audience, 'that I must truly become as I was. The master *bandito* of *antano.* That mean long ago, *gringo.* Like you say, yesteryear. And while I am seeking you, *senorita,* I discover that others are doing the same. And I discover that your very rich father, he puts the value of five thousand American dollars on your life.'

Once more, Don Benito Canales attempted to convey

without words a message he could only hope his daughter understood. And Steele could not spare the time – nor did he have the inclination – to find out if Rosa read what was in the eyes of her father. For his entire attention was concentrated upon Eduardo Riaz – with Canales seen on the periphery of the centre of his focus.

'In the American town of Phoenix in this Territory of Arizona, I know I am closer to finding you than is anybody else, *senorita.* And I send the telegraph to Don Benito Canales. That if he wishes to see his daughter soon, he should come the way I have come. I do not use my own name for this, of course. You understand so far, *senorita*?'

'*Si*,' Rosa forced out.

'*Bueno.* I do not need to go to the military town of Fort Curry: to know that you have gone there. I know there is just the one crossing of the Rio Colorado that you can use and I cross ahead of you. But I am not so young as when I was the smartest bandit in all of Mexico. I fall and injure my *tobillo* . . . for the *gringo* – '

'Ankle,' Don Benito Canales supplied automatically.

'*Si.* So I must rest. I hear the gunshot close to the river, but I am in no position to see what has happened. I can only rest and wait. Then, when I am well enough to follow your sign again, I think I am too late – that the Apaches have you and my plan is no good. But I follow the sign, still, hoping I will be lucky. And the rest, you know, yes?'

He grinned his pride in past achievements and shifted the gaze of his bright eyes from Rosa Canales to Adam Steele and back again.

'You reckoned it would be easier for you if I took care of Rosa on the way home – less trouble for you?'

'Of course. But I always keep the eye on you. At the river, where the man she had shot attempted to take his revenge, I would have kept her safe had you failed, *gringo.* I do not know what happened in Fort Curry. But I see one of two men I know are hoping for five thousand dollars riding in the desert near there. And I kill him.'

'For the hell of it, feller?'

'*Quisa,*' he replied with a slight shrug. 'You will recall it had been long time since I learn of Claudio's death and I become as I once was. And I had not killed anybody.'

'You didn't blast him with that little gun you have in your hand, feller?'

A shake of the head, with his grin widening. 'That is right, *gringo.* With my rifle from a great distance. The long range shot, yes?'

'After spotting him with field glasses, maybe?'

'Field glasses?' Riaz was momentarily puzzled. Then he shook his head again and got the grin back on his face. 'I know. No, with the telescope. You know?'

He raised his free hand to his face, and formed it into a loose fist which he briefly rested against an eye.

'The glass of this is what we saw in the sun, Adam?' Rosa Canales said, so caught up in the exchange between the two men she perhaps even forgot that the most important – to her – purpose it served was to delay the moment when Riaz intended to kill her.

'After another killing for the hell of it at the old stageline way station back along the trail?' Steele said, adding the query with an arching of his eyebrows.

Riaz looked away from the Canales father and daughter and the Virginian to direct a stream of saliva off the rig and on to the trail. But he was not distracted by a bad memory for long enough for Steele to even think about making a move against him.

'That *estupido gringo*? He is there, sleeping and snoring, when I reach the place. I could have ended his life there and then. But it amuses me to let him live for awhile. Especially when he tells me he has the intention of earning the reward put up by Don Benito Canales. It is amusing to me to pretend to be as *estupido* as is he. And to pretend that I am so impressed as I watch him and listen to him when you and the *senorita* come to the place. Then to blow off some of his head so I can see if he really has any brains at all, you know? That really took me back to the days of *antano,* you know? Yesteryear, uh?'

'Real fun,' Steele allowed sardonically. 'Then all you had to do was ride like a bat out of hell to fix up this meeting?'

'I know you knew of me, *gringo.* Of my presence like the ghost. That is what I was known as many years ago when I was the *bandito.* The *federales* call me *El Espectro.* It amuses me, too, *gringo* – to reveal myself to you in such a way as I did. So that you are too surprised to take the action. The *tactica de sorpresa,* uh?'

'Shock tactics, *senor,*' Don Benito Canales translated dully.

'That how he got the upper hand of you and your men, feller?' Steele asked, seeing the concern deepening the lines in the man's face and sensing his daughter's expanding anxiety as the braggart neared the end of his account and time began to run out fast.

'Cunning, *gringo*!' Eduardo Riaz snapped before his prisoner could even start to formulate an answer. 'I already tell you I have sent the telegraph to him to go to this part of the country. In the hills of the Gila Bend this afternoon, I am able to watch you and the *senorita* coming from the west – through the telescope, as you guess. And, as the luck would have it, Canales and his men are coming from the east. When the time is right, I need only to show myself, say I am the man who sent the message and . . . well, *gringo,* once I am close enough to this *hombre* to threaten him so – ' He stabbed the revolver muzzle harder into the flesh under the left ear of his prisoner. ' . . . I have no trouble with his men. Especially when I tell them in all honesty, that I have the intention to kill the daughter and not the father. I do not think Rosa Canales is much loved by the employees of De Raza Hacienda.'

He sighed, looked thoughtful for a few moments and then went on: 'I think all has been told now. For the *senorita* to understand and for the *gringo* to know how he has been made the *tonto.* The sucker, yes? But Don Benito is Mexican, the same as I. And we Mexicans, we are men of honour who keep our words. Don Benito promised to pay five thousand dollars American to whoever brings his daughter to him and this I am certain he will do. And I say I will take from him what he has taken from me. So that he may grieve as I must for all that is left of our lives. My promise I now keep.'

'Rosa, *perdoner* – ' Don Benito Canales started, but made no move to distract Riaz.

'*Papa*!' was all that his daughter managed to force out before the sobs hit her.

'You're the kind of greaser gets all greasers a bad name, Pancho,' the Virginian drawled, dragging his clawed right hand up and down along his right thigh – like he had just developed a bad itch. This as he remained apparently easy in the saddle, impassive faced as he spoke the kind of remark that a half Mexican he had run into a couple of times would have killed him for making. Nothing about his demeanour that indicated he was sweating on this full Mexican not being quite so touchy on the subject as the man named Edge – who would not have asked for qualification before killing.

'*Gringo*?' Eduardo Riaz growled, frowning into ugliness.

'The kind that has a head as big as his ass,' Steele went on, scratching his knee now. Then moving his clawed hand down his calf. 'And from what I hear coming out of your mouth, it's filled with much the same material.'

When Eduardo Riaz had been the most feared bandit in Mexico and was called *El Espectro* he probably would not have fallen for the ploy the Virginian used. And now, even after many years of well-heeled retirement from the hard life, he was only taken in for a second.

Which happened to be just long enough for Adam Steele. Who had been sick for a short time but was now fully recovered – and in a mood to prove to himself that his confidence as well as his health was restored.

The small calibre revolver in the Mexican's fist had only

ever been intended as a visible threat to Don Benito Canales. Who was not scheduled to die. So the suddenly angrily insulted Riaz needed a longer range weapon with which to kill Rosa Canales. Before the *gringo* became for that vital second the more urgent target.

Riaz started to bend his legs and reach for his rifle that looked like it could be resting on the phaeton's rumble seat. And, as he did so, the pressure of the revolver's muzzle against the flesh of Canales was eased.

Steele plunged his hand in through the slit in his pants leg and fisted it around the knife in the boot sheath. Drew the knife from the sheath and out of the slit.

Perhaps a half second had elapsed since Riaz had realised he had been fooled into an enraged move: while he struggled to guard against the impulse to panic – and lost. Saw the knife in the Virginian's hand and knew he had no time to line up a one-handed shot with his rifle. So swung the revolver – away from the head of Canales to aim it at Steele. Which was the moment when Canales should have played a part in his own salvation and that of his daughter. Which was maybe what Rosa started to scream at him to do, Steele thought, as he wrenched back his arm and then swung it forward: making allowances for the fact that he was hurling himself sideways off the stallion as he directed the knife on its spinning way.

Don Benito Canales remained seated as rigidly as a statue, and was as silent. Rosa Canales stood in the stirrups, like she thought the extra height would add urgency and authority to whatever it was she yelled at her father – in a voice so shrilly loud it almost masked the crack of Eduardo Riaz's revolver. Adam Steele crashed to the hard packed dirt of the trail and even he did not know for sure whether he had been hit by the small calibre bullet. For the pain of the deliberate fall totally filled his awareness of sensation. In much the same concentrated manner as his eyes saw clearly only the Mexican with the handgun and his ears strained to pick up what Riaz was snarling against the shrieking voice of the woman.

The range was too long for the handgun to be effective, unless by some chance the bullet was steered into a vital area of the target. Which Riaz should have recognised at the outset – and ducked into the cover of his hostage while he went for his rifle.

By the same token, the range was also too long for the knife to cause serious damage – for although in the skilled hands of the Virginian it was started out along an accurate path, it lacked the speed of a bullet and lost penetrating power with every inch it travelled. Which, as the instigator of the move, Adam Steele had taken into account. So that his dive from the horse was never intended as a means of dodging the bullet. Instead, to get his hands back on the Colt Hartford.

Rosa suddenly curtailed her angry and terrified plea to her father. And the string of fast spoken Spanish curses vented by Riaz could now be heard. This as the one time bandit chief did now duck, and leaned to the side at the same moment. To evade the spinning knife that went over his shoulder and started to arc down to the trail behind the stalled rig. Steele recognised only the words *gringo* and *Americano*, but was aware of the man's tone of voice altering from anger to triumph.

Then, though, there was just the violent din of rifle fire. That either covered or curtailed all other sounds. As the Virginian, sprawled full length in the prone position, by turns thumbed back the hammer and squeezed the trigger of the Colt Hartford. The rifle angled slightly upwards, to explode bullets among the legs of the white team horses, under the seat of the phaeton where Canales remained as unmoving as ever, through the open framework of the skeleton struts and into the other Mexican who stood on the footboard of the rig's rumble seat.

One bullet into each knee. Then another two at the same targets. Which was when Eduardo Riaz sat down hard on the seat, his feet slipped off the board and he dropped through the skeleton frame. His belly was presented as a target and Steele fired a fifth shot into it. Then expended the final bullet from the cylinder of the revolving rifle into the chest of Riaz, left of centre. So that the man was dead and spared further agony as his bullet-shattered form crumpled into a heap beneath the elegant rig with its wealthy driver still looking as inert as a corpse himself.

'*Madre de Dios*,' Rosa Canales gasped as she lowered herself back into her saddle.

'Mother of God, I expect you know, *senor*?' Don Benito Canales said slowly, his voice as dead of tone as was his face of expression.

'Sure,' Steele confirmed as he rose cautiously to his feet, grimacing as bruised flesh protested – but certain he had not been even nicked by the single shot from the handgun.

The five horses and the burro had been unsettled by the explosive violence that had lasted for perhaps ten seconds. Now they remained quiet, unmoving and tense – ears pricked high for an audible sign of further trouble and nostrils flared to the diminishing taint of drifting gunsmoke. But they were not made any more uneasy as their bulging eyes watched the Virginian get to his feet and move along the trail. Only the Canales father and daughter were perturbed as they watched him. And their tension was eased when they saw he had merely gone to retrieve his knife.

Rosa began to speak then, to her father in Spanish. And he nodded often and just occasionally spoke a word of agreement. This while Steele pulled his knife out of the trail and replaced it in the boot sheath, then went back to his horse: leaving in his tracks a trail of spent shellcases ejected from the chambers of the Colt Hartford. He had reloaded the rifle and slid it back into the boot by the time the bunch of men from De Raza Hacienda had started out from the hills – and their *patron* and his daughter had finished their secret talk.

'Kindly excuse our rudeness in excluding you from what has been said, *senor*,' Don Benito Canales said as Steele swung up into the saddle. Then he heard the far off beat of hooves and glanced over his shoulder toward the hills. And went on as he looked back at the Virginian and delved a hand into an inside pocket of his coat: 'Rosa would wish that you accompany us back to our home where both of us would enjoy having you stay for as long as you like. So that we may be able to express our gratitude to you in a less commercial way than this.'

He took from his pocket a sheaf of bills which he extended toward the Virginian.

'Rosa and I made a deal, feller.'

'I know. She has told me. There are here ten five hundred dollar banknotes, *senor.* You may have the money and come with us. Or you may have it and I will promise to send you any reasonable additional amount to whatever address you care to – '

He broke off as Steele heeled his horse to the side of the rig, and reached out a hand to take the money.

'Grateful, but a deal is a deal.'

'Adam, that was simply to take me home, was it not? You have saved the life of my father now and – '

'Rosa, there is nothing more to be said if that is how the American wishes it,' Don Benito Canales interrupted as his men slowed their mounts and then halted them in a tight knit group behind the rig. The riders and mounts were as neat and tidy as the man on the phaeton: the men as incurious as their horses – and their boss.

'Except, perhaps, *hasta la vista*, Adam?' Rosa suggested, her tone melancholic: since she knew it was a false hope.

The Virginian touched the brim of his hat with a forefinger and answered as he heeled the black stallion on to an arcing route around the group of other riders: 'Reckon it's more likely to be . . .

. . . *ADIOS.*'*

*But to readers of the series, it is just *hasta la vista* until Book No. 35 is published.